Lessons on how to piss off a lesbian serial killer:

1) Hit her in the head with the butt of a gun.
2) Treat her with disdain and underestimate her abilities.
3) Involve her family!

Alice awakens to discover she has been taken prisoner. Flashbacks are instantaneous, and when she realizes that Kathy and Emily are there too, she is compelled to return them to safety. Alice doesn't want her family involved in this part of her life. She isn't comfortable with them knowing, much less participating, after all her years of hard work to keep them in the dark.

Paybacks can be deadly for those who don't realize how truly gifted Alice is. Follow along as Alice continues to triumph at what she does so very well…

A K'Anne Meinel novel

Also by K'Anne Meinel:

Novels in Paperback:

SHIPS *CompanionSHIP, FriendSHIP,*
RelationSHIP
Long Distance Romance
Children of Another Mother
Erotica
The Claim
Bikini's Are Dangerous
The Complete Series
Germanic
Malice Masterpieces 1
The First Five Books
Represented
Timed Romance
Malice Masterpieces 2
Books Six through Ten
The Journey Home
Out at the Inn
Shorts
Anthology Volume 1
Lawyered
Malice Masterpieces 3
Books Eleven through Fifteen
Blown Away
Blown Away
The Alternate Cover

Small Town Angel
Pirated Love
Doctored
Veil of Silence
Malice Masterpieces 4
Books Sixteen through Twenty
The Outsider
Pirated Heart
Recombinant Love
Survivors
Inn the Dog House
Flight
An Island Between Us
Malice Masterpieces 5
Books Twenty-One through Twenty-Five
Malice Masterpieces 6
Books Twenty-Six through Thirty
Beauty and the Beast

Vetted Series:
Vetted
Cavalcade (Prequel)
Pioneering (Prequel)
Vetted Further
Vetted Again

Novellas in Paperback:

Sapphic Surfer
Sapphic Cowgirl
Sapphic Cowboi
Sayyida
The Northwood Lodge

The Malice Series:
Mysterious Malice (Book 1)
Meticulous Malice (Book 2)
Mistaken Malice (Book 3)
Malicious Malice (Book 4)
Masterful Malice (Book 5)
Matrimonial Malice (Book 6)
Mourning Malice (Book 7)
Murderous Malice (Book 8)
Mental Malice (Book 9)
Menacing Malice (Book 10)
Minor Malice (Book 11)
Morally Malice (Book 12)
Morose Malice (Book 13)
Melancholy Malice (Book 14)

Mad Malice (Book 15)
Macabre Malice (Book 16)
Marinating Malice (Book 17)
Macerating Malice (Book 18)
Minacious Malice (Book 19)
Meddlesome Malice (Book 20)
Meandering Malice (Book 21)
Maniacal Malice (Book 22)
Monitoring Malice (Book 23)
Marked Malice (Book 24)
Mandating Malice (Book 25)
Methodical Malice (Book 26)
Malevolent Malice (Book 27)
Militarial Malice (Book 28)
Machiavellian Malice (Book 29)
Malefic Malice (Book 30)

Religious Experience
Lied

All Novels and Novellas in paperback are also available as e-books.

Novellas in Paperback Continued:

A Woman Down Under Series:
Shanghaied (Prequel)
Outback Born
Outback Bred
Outback Heritage

Outback Native
Outback Splendor
Outback Yearnings (Prequel)
Outback Escape

Pocket Paperbacks:
Mysterious Malice (Book 1)
Sapphic Surfer
Sapphic Cowgirl
Meticulous Malice (Book 2)
Mistaken Malice (Book 3)
Malicious Malice (Book 4)
Masterful Malice (Book 5)
Matrimonial Malice (Book 6)
Mourning Malice (Book 7)
Murderous Malice (Book 8)

Mental Malice (Book 9)
Menacing Malice (Book 10)
Minor Malice (Book 11)
Morally Malice (Book 12)
Morose Malice (Book 13)
Melancholy Malice (Book 14)
Mad Malice (Book 15)
Macabre Malice (Book 16)
Marinating Malice (Book 17)

In E-Book Format:
Short Stories
Fantasy
Wet & Wet Again
Family Night
Quickie ~ Against the Car
Quickie ~ Against the Wall
Quickie ~ Over the Couch
Mile High Club
Quickie ~ Under the Pier
Heel or Heal
Kiss
Family Night 2
Beach Dreams
Internet Dreamers
Snoggered

On the Parkway
Stable Affair
Kept
Stolen
Agitated
Love of my LIFE
Quickie in an Elevator,
GOING DOWN?
Into the Garden
The Book Case
The Other Women
Menage a WHAT?

LARGE Print Novels
SHIPS CompanionSHIP, FriendSHIP,
RelationSHIP
Erotica Volume 1
Long Distance Romance
Children of Another Mother
Bikini's Are Dangerous
The Complete Series

Malice Masterpieces
The First Five Books
To Love a Shooting Star
The Claim
Represented
Timed Romance

K'ANNE MEINEL

Malefic

Malice

ISBN-13: 978-1959436072

K'Anne Meinel is available for comments at KAnneMeinel@aim.com as well as on Facebook, Google +, or her blog @ http://kannemeinel.wordpress.com/ or on Twitter @ kannemeinelaim.com, or on her website @ www.kannemeinel.com if you would like to follow her to find out about stories and book's releases.

www.shadoepublishing.com

ShadoePublishing@gmail.com

Shadoe Publishing is a United States of America company
Cover by: K'Anne Meinel
Edited by: Deb Amia

Malefic Malice

PUBLISHER'S NOTE

MALEFIC MALICE

Book 30

"Didn't anyone analyze her computers when they confiscated them?"

One of the techs who had been analyzing data started to laugh.

"What's so funny?"

"Yes, they did analyze her computers, the only one they were able to get into. This report herrrre…" he said, dragging out the word as he searched for the report in question, "states that not only are the computers encrypted, but you have to specify which country or countries in order to be able to get into the computer."

"What does that mean?"

"It means she has a helluva computer setup, and the encryption is impossible to break unless you have one person trying hundreds, possibly thousands, of variations and making no mistakes to access the data. Even

then, they have to declare the country she went through to obtain it or identify what country you accessed to find it."

"So, we can't read what was on her computers?"

"It was probably out of date anyway. She doubtless wiped it and then overwrote it just in case someone smarter than she got on them. I'm certain the police and the IRS tried a lot of things to get into them. This is a copy of the police report, and this one…" he pulled out a multi-page report, "from the IRS states that there was no way to break into these computers." He started to laugh again as he reread a section, "This one states they thought they had broken the encryption only to have the computer program start laughing loudly at them, the volume rising and falling and the voices calling them dirty names in various languages."

"Dirty names?" he asked, intrigued.

"I read that one," Madelyn put in, smiling at Alice's inventiveness. "Didn't the computer make seductive comments like, 'C'mon, baby, press my buttons some more' and 'Oooh, baby, did you have to bang my hard drive like that?' What about the one that screeched, 'What did you do to my floppy drive?'"

The group erupted in laughter.

"So, this Alice Weaver has a sense of humor?"

"Not only that. She obviously knew that someone would break the encryption at some point or think they had, and she prepared for it."

"She planned for it?"

Madelyn laughed as she nodded. They were finally getting the gist of the frustration she had felt many times while trying to investigate Alice Weaver years ago. They weren't going to find much. Alice was too good, too slippery, and now, she was certain she had the U.S. government by the short hairs. There was more that Alice knew and wasn't telling. Madelyn

knew the powers that be might just get fed up and send in a team to capture Alice, and that would be fatal. She was certain Alice had planned for this possibility and had things set up in the event of her demise. They couldn't afford the bad press; it would give the government a pair of black eyes. They had to be careful and cooperative and hope Alice might give them additional information since they were literally coming up against dead ends. Almost all the players that Alice had given them were dead. Madelyn only hoped she could keep her superiors from losing patience.

They weren't going to get anything from Alice for the time being…she was a bit tied up.

* * * * *

Alice came to slowly, the headache forewarning her that she had been struck on the head. For a moment, she was back in that Central American prison, then confusedly, she was somewhere in Russia, but she realized that something was off. She started to focus. Looking about, squinting, she saw that she was in chains. Her wrists were bound to the chair arms, her legs to the bottom of the chair, and the ankle cuffs were painful where they rubbed against her bare skin.

She looked farther into the room. She saw Emily first, looking frightened and dirty, her hair down and bedraggled. Emily cast a stricken look at Alice and was relieved to see her mother conscious. Alice looked to the right and saw her wife, who was looking horrible. Kathy had a split lip, her skin pale beneath her dark hair, and she looked at Alice with bleary, tear-filled eyes, glancing at their daughter and back towards Alice.

"Alice Weaver?" a voice said in her ear, and Alice groggily looked up and focused on the too-close face of Artum. She smiled slightly, not

surprised. "I see you are awake finally," he sneered. "I want my money, and I want it now," he said in what he thought was an intimidating voice. The man behind him shifted uncomfortably.

Alice swallowed, trying to stimulate saliva flow and blinking her eyes rapidly to not only focus but also try to calm her aching head. Instead, she found herself gagging and heaving as she tried not to throw up from the migraine she was experiencing.

Artum backed away in case she threw up on his expensive shoes, looking at the blonde woman in disgust. He glanced at the two men behind him in amusement before looking back at Alice. For such a petite woman, she had been a huge pain in the ass. He didn't believe everything Sebastian had warned him about, but he believed enough of it that he had developed a newfound respect for her. However, he had captured her, and she was helpless before him.

Alice had seen Artum's legs back away as she gagged. She glanced around the room, assessing it. They were in some sort of basement. It was made up to look like a dungeon. She wondered at that, betting it was the bottom floor of Sebastian's (now Artum's) mansion. The man lacked imagination. She'd seen that in all his operations she had studied and inventoried. He was a thug with no ideas of his own, living off Sebastian's carefully built empire and expanding in very obvious, patterned ways. Sebastian had been sophisticated and elite, and he kept his more unsavory business dealings separate from his legitimate business. Artum had completely blurred the lines separating the unsavory and legitimate. Alice finally raised her head, eyeing the man who was dressed to go out in a fine, pinstriped, double-breasted suit, cutting his figure close. She supposed he was handsome in his own way. She kept her eyes heavy-

lidded, so he wouldn't realize how alert she really was. Plus keeping her eyes partially closed helped with the ache in her head.

"You have cost me a pretty penny, and I want the funds back," he hissed at her, leaning forward with one hand tucked inside his suit in the front, the other in his pocket. Alice supposed it was his attempt at looking debonaire.

"I don't know what–" she began, but he backhanded her, striking with the hand that had been in his suit front. Spit and snot flew as her head careened sideways. The migraine was excruciatingly painful, and she saw stars.

"Don't lie to me!" he spat in her face, grabbing her jaw and forcing her head up. "I know it was you who burned down my warehouse. The whores I caught told me!"

Alice smiled at him, allowing the humor to enter her eyes. She wasn't aware that her eyes had begun to change color, taking on an orange hue. She'd known that not all those women would get away. The drugs they had inhaled had probably inhibited their ability to flee. She wondered if any had escaped completely. She hoped so, for their sakes.

"You are going to replace every dollar you cost me," he informed her, "with interest!"

"I don't have–" she began, but he hit her again, not letting her finish. She glared at him. The orange of her eyes turned almost a shade of red, and he took an involuntary step back. "Takes a real man to hit a woman who is tied up," she told him conversationally, slurring it slightly around the blood flowing from her mouth.

"You are going to transfer twenty-five million dollars to me–" he began but was interrupted by the entrance of a Russian-speaking man.

"Kiev is on the line, sir," the man informed him, and Artum's head came up instantly. He unconsciously slicked back his hair as he straightened and neatened his appearance.

"Take over for me here. Get her account number and have her make the transfer," he told the man in Russian.

"Yes, sir," the man replied.

Alice watched the interplay in a mirror on one wall. It was obvious to her it was a two-way mirror…not a particularly good one at that. There was a light on inside the room, and she could tell someone was on the other side. She listened as Artum left, showing no sign that she understood what they had been saying. It had taken a moment for her to realize they were speaking Russian, but what Sasha had taught her came back quickly. The slang and dialect were easy for her to interpret.

"Unlock the shackles, and pull her up," the man ordered, standing in front of Alice to face her. He switched to English as he examined her and asked, "You know how to do a money transfer?"

Alice raised an eyebrow, this simple act causing her head to throb. She needed aspirin very soon. She played along and nodded, regretting the impulse as her head pounded.

"Good, I'll have a computer brought to you, and you will transfer the funds from your account to my boss' account," he told her reasonably.

"Why?" she rasped, allowing the blood that had pooled in her mouth to drool out as she wasn't willing to swallow it. The smack she'd received had caused one of her newer teeth to cut into her soft skin.

The man removing the shackle from one of her legs stepped back before the drool could drip on him. He looked at her disgustedly as he moved to the other leg, removing the heavy metal from around her ankle.

"I will treat you humanely, and you will be reasonable, no?" he asked.

"No," she answered agreeably.

He frowned. "You don't cooperate, and we will hurt you in ways you haven't even thought of," he threatened.

Alice laughed; he obviously didn't know her.

"You think this is funny?" He gestured to the other two men. It was then that Alice saw one of the men was Iggy, the man she had been looking for. He smiled at her when she noticed him, knowing full well that she had been seeking him. His companions had died, but he had been too smart for her. He approached Emily and stood behind her chair. The other man went directly to Kathy and pulled her head up, grasping at her long, brown hair. When her hair came out in his hand, he looked up, horrified, at the man standing in front of Alice and showed him the locks. "What is this?" the man asked, looking from his man to Kathy and back at Alice.

"Cancer," Kathy rasped out in pain, glancing at Alice and shaking her head. She could see the orange eyes even if these men could not.

Alice noticed her wife's bedraggled look, the wisps of hair hanging down and looking greasy and unkempt. She wondered how long they had been here and what the men had done to her wife and daughter.

"Doesn't matter," the man in charge said, nodding to the men.

The man behind Kathy grabbed more hair, and although much of it came out in his grasp, some of it remained attached, and it hurt. Alice could see the pain in Kathy's eyes as he pulled her head up.

"Noooo," Emily moaned as Iggy began to feel her up, squeezing her tender, young breasts painfully.

Alice's eyes darted between her wife and her daughter, then up at the man in front of her. Her leg lashed out. He was too close, and the heel kick she had intended for his kneecap took him down instead of knocking

him back as she had hoped. Too late, her knee came up and hit him in the crotch instead of in the face as she had planned. He went down like a shot, rolling away from her as he grabbed himself and moaned.

"Sergei!" the man holding Kathy called, alarmed.

The man on the floor held up his other arm, nodding. He was unable to speak but wanted to cut off whatever the other man was about to say.

"Nooo," Emily was saying again and again as she twisted and tried to pull herself away from Iggy's roving hands while he whispered in her ear. He reached down to pull her legs apart and began feeling at the apex of her jeans. Alice's eyes glittered as she watched the picture before her.

Sergei gently pulled himself up and called, "Iggy!" to distract the man. He had been able to hear the young man even if Alice hadn't.

Iggy looked up, unaware that Sergei had fallen to the ground. He let the young woman go and went to help Sergei up. Sergei grasped his arm tightly, and Iggy lifted him from his prone position. Slowly, Sergei straightened as he breathed through his nose, taking great cleansing breaths.

"Sorry about that. It wasn't intentional," Alice assured him, feeling a little better even though her head still throbbed. It must be the surge of endorphins helping to clear her head, but she still wanted to throw up and wondered how long she had been out.

"You...are...sorry?" he rasped out as the pain subsided slightly. Without another thought, he lifted his left leg and kicked between her legs. He was wearing cockroach killer boots, the ones with pointed toes used to catch bugs in a corner and prevent them from getting away. The only thing that saved Alice from real harm was the fact he used his left foot and not his right, which was still throbbing from the kick to his knee. He also

hadn't measured the distance properly and barely grazed her leg and crotch area with his boot.

Alice pretended the blow had been substantial and leaned over as though in tremendous pain. It hurt, but not like she had been expecting; her head hurt way worse.

"You bitch!" he rasped out in Russian. "You fucking whore!"

"Sergei, don't forget what Artum wants," the man holding Kathy reminded him.

Sergei nodded, his hand waving away the concern. "I treat you with respect, and you attack me?" he said to Alice in English.

She looked up, trying to look at him innocently and failing. The orange eyes were mere slits, evidencing her disdain for him. She wouldn't be surprised if there was a cut in her jeans from the point of those boots. She was just grateful he had misjudged his kick, or she'd be in a world of more hurt than she already was.

"We will continue this soon," Sergei ordered, bobbing his head towards his two comrades and the door. Slowly, he hobbled toward the door as they joined him. The man that had been holding Kathy's hair released it, shaking his hand as the long strands came away and fell to the floor.

Alice watched the strands fall as she thought about their situation. Twenty-five million wasn't much by her estimate, but Artum didn't know what she knew about his operations, and she had the books Richard Pasternack had been cooking. Artum also didn't have the money he thought he did as she knew where it was. She wondered if he realized how much Richard had blabbed before he died?

"You okay, Alice?" Kathy asked from where she sat, her gaze taking in the gobs of hair on the floor as she also checked out her daughter, who was sobbing in her chair, and Alice, who was bent over.

"Yeah, I'll be okay in a minute," Alice told her as she took a deep breath and looked up. "How long was I out?"

"Two days," Kathy informed her.

"Two days? Are you sure?"

Kathy nodded, her head looking oddly mishappen where the hair had been bunched up and pulled out.

Alice glanced at Emily. "You okay?" she asked when she caught the young girl's teary eyes.

"He hurt me," she sobbed.

Alice nodded. "I know. I'm sorry. This is all my fault. I'll get–"

"How is this your fault?" Kathy asked.

"I should have gotten you all out of the house sooner. We shouldn't have waited. Where's Sean?"

"He went over to a friend's house."

"Yeah, but what happens when he comes home and doesn't find us there?"

"He'll go back to his friend's house, thinking he can," Kathy finished for her.

Alice nodded and closed her eyes briefly at another wave of pain.

"Headache?" Kathy asked, knowingly.

"Yeah," Alice managed to get out through clenched teeth.

"I'm not surprised. They hit you with a rifle butt."

That explained the horrific pain she was feeling. She wished she could raise her hand to feel her head. "How about you?" she asked her wife instead and glanced at Emily, who was still sobbing slightly but was trying to get it under control.

"I'm okay. They just grabbed me, but I couldn't understand what they were saying. Was that Russian?"

Alice nodded, regretting the gesture immediately as she closed her eyes and said, "Yes."

"Did you–?" Kathy began, and Alice again answered, "Yes."

"You understood them?" she managed to finish her question this time.

"Yes," the blonde said a third time, trying to get the pain in her head under control, taking cleansing breaths through her nose and out her mouth.

The door opened, and the man who had grabbed Kathy's hair returned. "I'm going to feed the three of you," he informed them, wheeling in a trolley. He left it in front of Kathy, untying her first before moving towards Emily, who flinched away, but he determinedly untied her. They both looked at Alice, who had opened her eyes. She nodded at them to indicate they should start eating. "I'll untie you after they have eaten," he told her, giving her a wide birth as he eyed her feet. Sergei wasn't happy and was icing his balls upstairs. Artum had gone out after the phone call.

Kathy pulled the cover off the dish of food and gestured at Emily to join her. It was pork chops in gravy, mashed potatoes, peas, and a side dish of apple sauce. Alice shook her head at the drink she saw Kathy reaching for, and her wife immediately pulled her hand back, brushing Emily's hand aside as she reached for her own glass. Emily looked at her mother, then glanced over at her other mother, who shook her head slightly before closing her eyes again as she used meditation and cleansing breaths to try to lessen the ache in her head.

It took them a while to eat, and they were both still thirsty with nothing to wash down their food. They wondered why Alice wouldn't let them drink.

"Aren't you thirsty?" the man finally asked Kathy.

"We don't drink with our meals. It's bad for you to wash down a perfectly good meal," Kathy lied, knowing it was true but not something they practiced.

"I have to tie you up again," he told her, not unkindly.

"I…um…need to use the facilities," Kathy admitted.

"Pee in that corner," he said, pointing to the far wall. "There is a hole there that drains out."

"Seriously?" Emily asked. She too had to go.

"This isn't the Hilton," he said with a sneer. "Hurry up!"

Kathy exchanged a look with Emily, and they both glanced at Alice, who had a slight smile on her face but hadn't opened her eyes during their entire meal. Kathy shrugged and got up stiffly, heading for the corner. She was surprised to see a roll of toilet paper. They hadn't been fed since they got here, but that didn't mean she hadn't felt an urge to go in those two days; she'd just suppressed it. The thought of relieving her bladder suddenly made it harder to hold, and she quickly squatted, unfastening and pulling down her jeans. She was embarrassed when the man didn't look away and watched her. Hearing herself pass gas mortified her, and Emily, who had been following, turned around to give her mother some privacy. She glared at the man. The food had given her some time to overcome the humiliation of the other man's touch. She remembered him doing the same thing at Christmas last year too. She remembered him, and she wished him dead.

"Here…your turn," Kathy murmured to Emily as she wiped herself and got up, pulling her pants up and fastening them again.

"There's nowhere to wash our hands," Emily murmured in complaint.

"Do the best you can," Kathy told her as she stood in front of her fastidious daughter protectively, blocking the man's amused look at their discomfort.

In no time at all, they were tied up on the chairs again, and Alice was now allowed to eat. The metal cover had kept her meal warm, and she enjoyed the two pork chops and savored the gravy on her potatoes. She eyed the fork she was using, wondering if she could use it to kill the man fast enough but deciding to wait until her meal was done. She hoped the food would help with her headache. As the man leaned forward on the table, tired of waiting for the third prisoner to finish eating, she acted without waiting another moment.

"You ever seen this?" she asked, rapidly moving the fork in and out between his splayed fingers quickly and accurately, while just missing his fingers with the prongs. His eyes were captivated by the gesture, and before he could react, she turned the fork and deftly shoved it up the center of his nose, breaking the cartilage with the force of her blow and shoving the prongs into his brain. She thrust him backwards as she grabbed the edge of the dish cover and used it like a blade. As he went down, she sliced across his neck, hitting his jugular and jumping back before the blood spurted all over her. He was dead in moments.

"Holy shit, Alice!" Kathy said, losing her dinner. She was immediately followed by Emily, who also threw up at the sight of the dead man and the smell of her mother vomiting.

"Come on you two," Alice said, trying to keep her displaced humor in check. She quickly frisked the dead man, coming up with only a pocketknife. Alice untied them, using the knife when necessary. She threw each of the women the dainty cloth napkin that had been included with their meal, so they could wipe at their bile-speckled mouths.

"How did you know the drink was drugged?" Kathy asked as she wiped her lips. She just had gotten a glimpse of herself in the two-way mirror and was horrified to see the clumps of hair missing from her head. There was no way to hide the bald spots.

Alice shrugged. "Just a guess."

"Well, that was a meal well wasted," Kathy put in as she dropped the napkin on the wheeled cart. Emily followed suit, her eyes taking in the fork protruding from the man's face, the severed neck, and the blood leaking across the floor in a widening pool. She wanted to throw up again but restrained herself…just barely.

"I'm feeling better," Alice confided as she headed for the door and glanced out. No guards. She guessed they didn't think they needed guards in their own house. "Stay close and keep quiet," Alice cautioned in a whisper as she went out the door.

It was a beautiful basement with large paving stones holding up the walls. Their rounded edges made them look old and sculpted. Alice headed for a set of stairs also constructed of the paving stones, which led upstairs in a curving arch to what looked like a kitchen. She briefly wondered how the man had gotten the trolley down into the basement as she looked around the door and saw Sergei sitting in a kitchen chair with his pants pooled around his ankles and a large bag of ice held against his crotch. He was leaning back, facing the ceiling, and his eyes closed in relief. She nearly laughed. Instead, she turned, signaling for Kathy to stay back. She crept into the kitchen, trying to stay out of Sergei's line of vision.

"Iggy, is that you?" Sergei called out. His voice was slightly slurred, and Alice now noticed the wine bottle next to his hand. She wondered if the man had heard her or was just calling out drunkenly to his friend. She

didn't pause as she reached the block containing several cutting knives and pulled out two. Hefting them in her hand, she balanced them, reversed them, and finally hurled one at the prone man. She was disappointed when she missed her mark. That was something that hadn't happened in years, but she wasn't going to worry about it right now. She let the second knife fly almost immediately.

Sergei heard the thump and felt the slight whiff of air as the first knife missed his throat by mere millimeters. The second knife didn't miss, and he looked up just as it struck him in the throat. He looked surprised to see Alice standing there. She was already reaching for another knife although she knew the second had hit home. He dropped the bag of ice he was holding to his balls as he lurched forward but made it no further as he fell to the floor. Alice took another knife anyway as she gestured to her wife and daughter.

"How did you–?" Emily began, but Kathy shushed her, grabbing her hand to pull her along. Alice looked around and found the back door, carefully unlocking it, then slowly opening it while gesturing for her wife and daughter to hurry up. She eased it open and looked around, seeing a backyard with a six-car garage and surprised to see her own Rover parked in the courtyard.

"Head for the car," she whispered to her wife. "I'm going to clean up in here," she gestured inside.

"No, I want to stay with you," Kathy stated, suddenly frightened.

"Me too," Emily answered, feeling argumentative.

"There are at least two men inside that I have to find, and with you along, I won't find them as quickly," Alice reasoned. "Get in the Rover and give me fifteen minutes. If I'm not there in fifteen minutes, start the car and go!"

"I'm not leaving without you," Kathy argued, weakly grabbing Alice's arm.

"Did you drink some of that stuff?" Alice asked, seeing Kathy's eyes were dilated.

"No, but I haven't had my meds in two days, and I bet some of them are giving me withdrawals," she said as she weaved on her feet.

"Shit," Alice mumbled, torn between helping her wife and avenging her loved ones.

"I'll get to the car," Kathy promised, suddenly realizing they'd be in the way, and Alice needed to hunt. These men couldn't be allowed to get away with what they had done to her family. She was feeling weak after the brief meal and the adrenaline surge that followed.

"I want to help," Emily tried to argue.

"Look, I need you to help your mom," Alice told her reasonably. "Please?"

Emily looked at Alice. Her mother had just killed two men and didn't even have a drop of their blood on her. Her actions had been cool, calm, and efficient. She realized that if she took care of Kathy, Alice would have free rein to search for the creep who had touched her. The filth he had murmured in her ears would haunt her forever. She nodded slightly as she realized Alice's eyes were practically glowing orange. She turned back to Kathy and took her arm, helping her down the back steps towards the Rover.

Alice breathed a sigh of relief as she carefully closed the door behind them, ensuring it made no noise.

* * * * *

They had waited five minutes. Kathy was in the driver's seat but feeling poorly. They had brushed off the seats before getting in as the broken glass from the windows was still covering them. Afterward, they sat down gingerly and waited. The food, the bile, and the lack of meds was catching up with Kathy. Sleeping in an awkward position last night while tied to a chair hadn't been good for her. Watching Alice and worrying that she wouldn't wake up hadn't helped things either. Kathy and Emily had attempted to talk but someone came in and threatened to gag them if they didn't shut up.

"Mom," Emily finally whispered, her hand pointing at a gas pump she noticed alongside the garage.

"What?" she asked just as silently, wondering what the teen was getting at.

"Let's cause some damage."

It took Kathy a moment to understand what Emily was talking about, but then, she got the idea. They both slipped from the car, and Kathy staggered a little on the cobblestones of the courtyard. She had to be careful; now, was not the time for a broken ankle. It was Emily who saw the basement window—maybe the window to the room they had been kept in—and she kicked the glass in. They looked around to see if anyone had noticed the noise, but when no one came, they proceeded with their plan. At first, they didn't think the gas hose would reach that far, but they found by unwinding all the twists, the nozzle just barely made it through the window bars. Emily wedged the nozzle between the bars and used a rock under the handle to hold it wide open. Kathy flipped the lever on the pump, and the liquid began pouring through the broken window. The air was soon filled with the odor of gasoline, and Kathy had a memory of the

time Alice explained to her that it wasn't the gasoline that burned but the vapors. They returned hurriedly to the Rover.

"Here, you get in the driver's seat," Kathy told her, feeling the last of her adrenaline wearing off as she got in the back seat.

"Are you sure?" the teen asked, suddenly feeling even more excited at being entrusted with the driving.

"I can't drive," Kathy admitted as she lay down on the back seat. "Stay down and make sure the passenger door is unlocked."

Emily did as she was told, pulling the lever to let her seat down and keep her out of their line of sight if anyone came looking. She raised up just enough to see out, keeping her eyes glued on the back door they had emerged from and mentally wishing Alice would come through it.

* * * * *

Alice found the living room they had been in, the one where even now a few of the Weaver possessions remained on the shelves. She was tempted to retrieve them but resisted. They'd gotten their insurance settlement, and if Kathy had wanted to replace any of these items, she probably already had. Artum was welcome to these ones. She began looking for Iggy and Artum.

She found Iggy on the second floor in a room near the master bedroom where Sebastian had died. Iggy was watching television—porn—and masturbating to what he was seeing on the screen. He never heard the door open as he was in the throes, his penis hard and erect, but he definitely felt the pain when Alice cut off his member, covering his mouth before he could scream. He stared in horror as she lifted the penis and held it in front of his shocked eyes before quickly shoving it into his wide-

open mouth. His hands came up to remove it, but she quickly stabbed through one hand, pinning it to the recliner he was sitting in. She used her weight to move the remaining hand back to the arm of the chair and pinned it with another knife. For a second, she watched as his fingers wiggled against the chair spasmodically, twitching as though in a fit. "You like little girls, Iggy?" she hissed, having witnessed him touching her daughter twice, the second time painfully. She glanced at the porn he had been watching and saw it was teenage girls, and she sneered at the castrated man with his blood oozing all over the expensive upholstery of the chair from between his legs. His pants were down to his knees, his middle fully exposed.

"No one touches my family and gets away with it. You may have hidden for a while, but everyone gets their comeuppance, you piece of filth. And don't think I didn't understand what you said to my daughter," she told him, her hearing excellent and her rage frightful. She repeated his words back to him in imperfect Russian, his eyes widening in horror as he had spoken to the girl in English, so she would understand what he planned to do to her. As he grew weak from blood loss, Alice finished her litany of his words and ended with, "And now, you eunuch, I will finish you!" When she pulled the pocketknife from her pants' pocket, he recognized it as his comrade's, and he watched in further horror as she cut off his balls, the sawing motion on his loose and bloody flesh causing excruciating pain. He screamed around the penis in his mouth. "Does that hurt, Iggy?" she taunted as she threw the flesh of his balls at the big screen where three men were pumping away at a girl. The blood splattered sickeningly across the screen. Alice wiped the blade on his shirt, the blood loss and horror of watching himself being mutilated leaving him too weak to struggle against the knives pinning his hands to the chair. She smiled in

his eyes as she deftly folded the dull blade of the pocketknife and slipped it into his shirtfront. Patting it, she departed, leaving him there with two kitchen knives fixing his hands to the chair, his lifeblood leaking out between his legs, his penis in his mouth, and his balls lying grotesquely on the floor where they had fallen down the big screen. His eyes were fastened on his balls, and he stared, not the big screen, but at the flesh on the floor as he died in the chair.

Alice saw guards outside walking the grounds as she looked out the windows, but Artum was nowhere to be found. That was...disappointing. She tripped no alarms as she searched the house, so they must have felt they were safe with just the guards. She made her way back downstairs, stopping on the first landing when she saw Sandy Pasternack picking up her handbag and leaving by the front the door. Her eyes narrowed musingly as she quickly made her way to the back door through the kitchen and slipped outside. She got a strong whiff of gas just as a guard came around the corner smoking a cigarette. Alice had no choice but to take him down when his gun came up.

She ran at him, glancing up at the corner of a small porch and making use of the aluminum bar that held the roof out to shed rain. She swung up, the aluminum bar bending under her weight, and wrapped her legs around the guard's neck, quickly twisting and turning at the same time. His hands came up to fend her off, causing him to drop his gun onto the cobbles of the courtyard with a clatter. Alice's twist cut off his oxygen supply, and using her weight, she fell on top of him with her legs crossed behind his neck to keep the tension on and choke him. She winced at the pain as he fell backwards onto her legs, but she kept up the tension, not releasing him as he choked and thrashed, pulling unsuccessfully at her legs. She looked

down at his flushed face and watched as he choked to death in her hold. She could feel herself weakening as he finally breathed his last.

"Mom, that was amazing," Emily gasped as she helped Alice up.

"Where did you come from?" she asked, letting the teen help her as her knee was badly bruised from the man's fall. "Do you smell gas?" she asked.

"Um, yeah. About that…" the teen began, helping a limping Alice towards the SUV.

Alice was surprised to find Kathy in the back as Emily helped her into the passenger seat. "Are you okay?" she asked Kathy worriedly.

"Nauseous. I need to get home," she answered. "Are you okay?"

"Yeah, just a bruised knee. How–?"

But Emily had closed the door, cutting off her question, and she was running around to get in the driver's seat.

"Oh, no…" Alice began, but the teen waved her protestations aside.

"Neither of you can drive, and we have to get out of here now!" the teen told her, her adrenaline riding high. Seeing Alice coming out the back door, she had quickly sat up in the seat, pulling the lever to bring it upright. Watching Alice attack the man that Emily hadn't even noticed, she had marveled at her mother's fluidity. This was nothing like the skirmishes she saw on television; it was better. She winced as the man went down under her mother's weight, then seeing the momentary look of pain on Alice's face, she had gotten out of the car. She nearly tripped on the cobblestones but had gotten there just as Alice finished the man off, so she could help her mother up. Emily had seen the glowing butt of the cigarette and the splashed gasoline, and she knew it was only a matter of time before the gas they had been pumping into the basement was found or the glow of that cigarette caused it to go up in flames.

Emily buckled her seat belt, reaching down to pull the seat forward, so she could reach the gas pedals comfortably. She told Alice to put on her belt as she started the car and slammed it into gear. As Alice began to argue with her strong-headed daughter, Emily quickly explained about the gasoline they had pumped into the basement. Alice had also seen the cigarette and smelled the gas, and she didn't need to be told twice. Emily was hesitant at first, but Alice encouraged her with, "Go, go, GO!" and they sped through the courtyard and onto the driveway, heading for the gate.

The gate was open, and Alice only briefly wondered if Sandi Pasternack had just gone through.

"Which way?" the teen fretted, worrying suddenly that they would get pulled over by the police. They'd never be able to explain away all the broken windows, and they didn't want any questions about anything else that had just occurred.

Alice pointed and watched as the teen uneasily made her way down one street and then another. The Rover rocked from side to side as the nervous teen drove carefully, ever conscious that her mothers were in the SUV with her. "Pull over here," Alice told her after a while, knowing there was no way Emily could cope with Los Angeles traffic at the moment.

Disappointed but also relieved, Emily deftly pulled over to the curb. She got out, intending to help Alice into the driver's seat, but her mother met her as she limped around the front. "You did good," Alice said, squeezing her arm as she painfully hobbled towards the open door. Alice got in, and they both buckled up just in time to hear the explosion and see the fireball from a couple blocks away. "Holy shit!" she murmured, unable to see it clearly with all the houses and trees between them, but she couldn't miss the smoke above the trees or the noise the explosion made.

Just as they emerged from the hilly area of Beverly Hills, they met fire engines pulling onto the main drag. Alice pulled over to allow the fire engines and a line of police cars with lights flashing and sirens blaring to pass as they headed up the hill. Alice drove sedately away from the area, heading for home and minding her own business.

* * * * *

That night on the news, there was a helicopter's view of the fireball that had once been Sebastian's home. The devastation was absolute. The house had burned hotly, and there was an ongoing investigation into the explosion. The reporter stated, "I hope no one was in there," but Alice they knew at least three people had been in there, and she secretly wondered if the fire had burned too hot for them to find the bodies, briefly musing that ash might be all they found with that heat.

The Rover was parked in the garage. Alice had arranged to have the smashed windows replaced later that week. They'd gotten home early enough that she had been able to make a few phone calls. They'd all showered, Kathy had taken her pills, they'd eaten, and now, they were sitting in the master bedroom relaxing. After watching the news, Kathy had turned off the television, so they could just chat and try to calm down after the events of the past two harrowing days.

"So, our gardeners are assassins?" Kathy asked, wonderingly.

Alice nodded. After a few key questions from Kathy, she told her family what had happened. There were no signs of the Russian lackeys that had rushed their estate. "I got the idea from the Ottomans. They always employed gardeners who were assassins and usually mutes. Instead, I chose men I felt I could trust and who would keep their mouths

shut despite anything they might see around here. I hired men who needed employment to get a green card, and this legitimized their work. Julio rotated his men."

"Who is Julio?" Kathy asked, forestalling Emily, who was listening avidly. She wasn't letting her mothers shut her out, not after what they had all been through. She was warm, dry, and wrapped in her cozy, velour bathrobe.

Alice shifted slightly, showing she was uncomfortable. The bruise on her knee was bad. She'd iced it, but she was out of shape for the moves she had made that day. She knew she would be sore for days. All the tension had washed away in the shower, and now, she was stiff. She was also listening for sounds that Sean was home. When they'd retrieved their phones from where they left them on the kitchen counter, she had called her son and asked when he was coming home. Getting back to her wife's question, Alice confessed, "Julio is a business acquaintance." She held up her hands in surrender at her wife's accusing glare. "He's only helping me out because he owes me."

"What exactly does he owe you for?"

"I gave him some of Artemis' business information, and he's been taking business away from the Russians."

"So, you are exchanging one drug dealer for another?"

"That's not how I see it," Alice admitted.

"But it's still drugs!"

"Yes, and eventually they will get caught!" Alice came back just as swiftly, feeling defensive.

"How?"

"Do you really want to know that?" she glanced from Kathy to Emily, who was watching, fascinated. Alice felt the young woman had a right to

some of this information and to know she was safe. Alice was certain she *was* safe but felt better now that they were home and cleaned up. She didn't know how long they were safe though, and she was worried that Sean wasn't home yet. Artum had really stepped over the line by taking both Kathy and their daughter. For now, they were home, and they were safe, but Alice desperately wanted to go hunting. She also wanted to know all her family members were out of harm's way. She was considering where they might go…where they might *have* to go.

She looked at Kathy, seeing her normally pale color from the drugs was back. At least she was no longer pasty-grey, the slight withdrawals she had felt already in check after getting back on her schedule of meds and eating a decent meal. The bald patches were rather prominent on her head now. She'd tried a combover, which was failing desperately, but Alice affected not to notice.

Kathy glanced at Alice's eyes darting back and forth between them for a moment before sighing and shaking her head. "I guess I don't really want to know how they will get caught," she admitted sadly.

"I do," Emily put in.

Alice smiled, turning toward her daughter. "No, believe me, it's better if you have deniability." She saw the teen ready to argue and put up her hand to forestall her. "If you are ever taken in for questioning by the authorities, the less you know, the better."

"I'd never tell on you!" she insisted.

"I know you wouldn't, darling, but there are interrogators that are top-notch at their jobs, and they would trick you. You don't know how to pass a lie detector test or how to avoid their traps, and I don't want you to."

"But—"

"Please trust me. There is a time and a place for everything, and I understand you are impatient. I was once like you, and you have to learn patience."

"After what he threatened to do to me?" she suddenly sobbed, using tears to manipulate her mother and get her to tell what she was planning.

"I heard what he said he would do to you, and he paid for his audacity in saying that to you and for touching you," Alice promised her.

"Did you kill him?" Emily stopped crying, looking up and fixing Alice with eyes just like her sister, Connie's. But now, her eyes were turning a shade that neither Kathy nor Alice had ever seen before.

"I don't think…" Alice began, trying to reason with her daughter, and then, she heard the front door open and close.

"Mom?" Sean called from the front hallway.

"We're up here!" Alice called back, anxious to see their son and assure herself that he was okay. To Emily she warned, "Not a word!" She glanced at Kathy, who nodded as she got more comfortable under the covers. She was exhausted. Alice unobtrusively covered her own bruised knee with her robe.

"Hey, thanks for letting me stay at Jeff's that extra night. I know, I know, it was a little much, but we…" he left off, seeing them all sitting on the bed and Kathy under the blankets. "Everything okay?" he worried. One side of Kathy's face looked a little red. He didn't realize the difference in her color, having not seen her for days. He also couldn't see that makeup was hiding the damage on both his mothers' faces.

"Your mom's been a little off, but she's feeling better," Alice answered truthfully, distracting him from looking too closely.

"Mom?" he asked Kathy, wondering if she was worse. She didn't look good to him. He could see her hair was thinning even more than he recalled, not realizing chunks of it had been pulled out.

"I'm fine. I threw up today, and it wasn't pleasant, but I just need a good night's sleep," she assured him.

He looked between his moms, wondering if they were keeping something from him, but he knew they'd always answer his questions if he asked. Right now, he didn't want to know the details about Kathy throwing up, and he wasn't sure he wanted to know anything else either. Her bodily functions didn't interest him in the least.

"So, are you some ninja warrior now with the video game?" Alice teased with her eyebrow raised.

"It's Warrior Call, Mom," he said in an exasperated voice as he grinned.

"Is that like Call of Duty?"

"Nope, completely different. You don't mind, do you?" he asked, not certain he wanted to stop playing the game even if she objected.

"Nope, so long as you keep up on your schoolwork and come up for air now and then. Don't let the gaming interfere with your sports either, okay?"

He smiled and leaned over to kiss her on the cheek. He moved to go over to Kathy's side of the bed, but the brunette waved him away. "I don't want you to get this if I have a cold or something," she warned him off. He was grateful.

"Hey there, squirt," he said, teasing Emily and poking her in the shoulder. Alice and Kathy saw her wince, but Sean didn't even notice as he made his way out the door. "I'm going to throw in a load of laundry. Anyone need anything washed?" he asked, hoping none of them did. He

didn't want to see any blood from female periods or anything Kathy might have thrown up on. He thought women's bodily functions were kind of gross.

"Nope, we're good," Alice told him with a smile. He was so easy to read, but she was pleased that he was at least trying. She knew he was a good guy and hoped he would stay that way. She smiled at Kathy, who had probably been the one to teach the kid how to do his own laundry. The sports he was involved in probably caused a lot of sweat, and he stank often.

They all waited until they heard him head down to the laundry, and then Emily hissed, "I should know what you did to that guy."

"Geez, Emily. Are you still on about that?" Alice asked, exasperatedly.

"Yes, I need to know," she said tenaciously.

"Are you ready to tell your mother what he whispered to you?"

"How did you hear that? You were farther away from me than Mom."

"Let's just say I read lips."

"Do you?" the teen asked, suddenly horrified at the things she had been caught out on over the years.

Alice just smiled and Kathy smothered a laugh. "Get some sleep, Emily. You are going to be sore tomorrow, and I think we are going to have plenty to talk about in the coming days," Kathy warned her.

"But Mommm," the teen whined, trying to wheedle some more information out of them.

Alice laughed. "No, m'dear, that's enough for now. Your mom is *tired*," she said meaningfully, and Emily took the hint.

"Oh, all right," she said dejectedly, wanting to know more but hoping their talks in the coming days would give her the information she

desperately wanted to know. She got up and gave Kathy a peck on the cheek, then came around to give one to Alice.

"Take some aspirin or ibuprofen before you go to sleep. It will help with the aches and pains you have now and the ones that are going to show up after you sleep in your bed."

Emily nodded as she turned and went through the door, closing it quietly behind her.

Alice looked at Kathy. "We won't be able to keep much from that one for long."

Kathy sighed. "No, we won't," she agreed. It saddened her how much Emily knew, or thought she knew, much less what the child had seen. She corrected herself mentally, *Emily was not a child. Not anymore.*

* * * * *

They woke up to earth-shattering screams coming from Emily's room. Alice leapt out of bed, opened their door and hobbled quickly down the hall followed much more slowly by an equally concerned and pained Kathy.

"What the hell?" Sean asked sleepily from his own doorway.

"I'm sure it was a nightmare," Kathy said as she came up. "You can go back to bed."

Alice was already in Emily's room. The normally neat room was a mess, and she looked about in concern, finally locating Emily on the floor, thrashing around and tangled in her blankets. She was screaming at the top of her lungs. As Alice caught her, she took a fist to her already battered head and winced as it connected in almost the same spot as the rifle butt. She'd hid her injuries from Sean, but careful concealer could

only do so much, and she had probably rubbed some off in her sleep. Holding her daughter carefully—tightly but not in a way that she could construe as someone holding her down—Alice crooned to her. "Emily...Em...Em. Wake up, honey. It's Mom. Shhh, shhh, shhh." She rocked the teen as she gently woke her. The girl seemed unusually deeply asleep, and Alice finally shook her hard. "Emily, wake up now. It's just a dream, honey. Wake UP!"

Emily blinked up at Alice, suddenly realizing the sense of her mother's words and hugging her tight. "Oh, God! Oh, Mommy!" she sobbed into Alice's shoulder.

Alice winced at how tightly the teen was holding her, but she held on, rocking her and shushing her. "It's okay, Em. I've got you and nothing's gonna get you. I've got you, baby. Shhhh." She glanced up at Kathy, who was standing in the door frame and using it to hold herself up. She was crying at seeing her daughter in so much pain.

"He was holding me down. He was...was..." she couldn't continue and started hiccupping as she sobbed. It took a long time for her to calm down.

"We're going to get you the therapy you need, darling. We'll help you," Alice told her and then looked up at a horrified Kathy, who shook her head. What could Emily tell a therapist? If Emily told anyone what she had seen or heard, they would all be arrested.

"Alice," Kathy called to get her wife's attention after looking down the hall to check that Sean had gone back to bed. The door was closed, and she was certain he was soundly asleep again. That boy needed his sleep; he was growing so much. "You are going to have to tell her what you did, so she can rest easier. She can't see a therapist; we all know that."

Alice nodded, realizing the truth of her words but reluctant to tell the teen more of her misdeeds. Holding her close, Alice closed her eyes and wished that Emily was five years old again and just holding her would be enough.

Finally, calming down enough to release the tight hold she had on Alice, Emily pulled back slightly. Kathy walked forward and handed her daughter a wet washcloth she had fetched from the bathroom to wipe her tears. "Here is a tissue," she also offered, so the teen could blow her nose. "Care to tell us what the dream was about?"

Emily shook her head. She didn't want to remember it and live it all over again. Thankfully, some it was already fading.

"You never have to worry about that man again," Alice promised the teen. "I took care of him, and I made sure he suffered."

Her eyes still awash with tears, Emily looked up into her mother's eyes. "Can you tell me what you did to him?" she asked hesitantly, sure that Alice would refuse her.

Alice sighed as she let the teen go and helped her back up on the bed, her own bruised and battered body making her slow and stiff. Straightening the bed sheets and covers in her agitation, she wanted to avoid telling the teen anything.

"Cleaning won't delay it for long," Kathy quipped, and Alice laughed, looking up at her wife knowingly. There was no fooling Kathy after all these years.

"When I went back upstairs looking for Iggy," she told the teen softly, keeping her voice down in case Sean was still awake, "I found him watching porn on a big screen TV." She glanced towards the door, and Kathy shook her head. She'd heard Sean's snores when she went to the bathroom for the cloth. "The porn he was watching was pretty much

everything he threatened to do to you. Before he knew I was there, I used one of the knives to cut off his cock." She watched as her daughter's eyes opened wider at the crude word. "I covered his mouth, so no one could hear his screams. Then, I shoved his penis in his mouth to gag him. As his hand came up to try and remove it, I pinned his hand to the chair with the knife, then I pinned the other hand with another knife."

"Wasn't he stronger than you?" the teen asked in awe as she visualized the man and what Alice was saying she had done to him.

"Yes, probably, but I had surprise on my side, and I'd waited until he was in the throes over watching what was on the screen." She had hoped she wouldn't need to get too graphic with her daughter and wasn't sure how much she already knew about masturbation or sex. "While he was pinned there and bleeding all over the upholstery, I asked if he liked little girls. I told him that no one touches my family and gets away with it. I also repeated exactly what he had said to you, only I said the words in Russian, and he stared, horrified, as he realized I had understood everything they had ever said. I could see the blood loss was affecting him. Next, I pulled out the pocketknife I had taken from the other guy and cut his balls off while he watched in horror. It was hard to do because that knife wasn't as sharp as the kitchen knives, but I managed. When I was done, I threw his balls against the big screen, leaving him to bleed to death. I also called him a eunuch," she smiled as she repeated that.

"What's a eunuch?" the teen naively asked.

"It's a man without a penis or sometimes just without balls," Kathy put in quietly, seeing how happy Alice was with what she had done on their daughter's behalf. Kathy was horrified but didn't feel as bad as she should have when she realized the man had threatened their daughter. "Exactly what did he say to you, Emily?" she asked, feeling sick.

Emily shook her head. She didn't want to remember. She was happy to know he was dead, but what Alice had done was horrifying, and she wanted time to think about it.

"Emily?" Alice asked, waiting for her daughter to look up. She realized she had been too graphic. She shouldn't have taken such pride in her work and repeated all the gory details to her wife and daughter. "Do I have your permission to tell Mom what he said?"

Relieved that she didn't have to repeat it, Emily nodded. "Just...not...now," she said in a voice that sounded exhausted.

Alice understood. She glanced at Kathy who nodded too. Looking back at Emily, Alice said, "I want you to know I'd do anything to keep you safe. I'm sorry they frightened you."

"It's okay, Mom. It's not your fault."

"Yes, Emily. This time it is my fault. I toyed with the man, and his minions came and took us. I should have handled it differently."

Emily looked up at Alice, surprised that she was taking the burden of this on her small, elegant shoulders. "It wasn't your fault, Mom. They decided what they would do, and they paid for it."

"Artum is still out there," Alice reminded her. "We have to be extra careful. I believe we are safe here...for now," she gestured at the house but wondered if they really were. The man's house had gone up in flames rather dramatically, and that might piss him off. He would want more than money this time; he was going to want revenge.

"Why don't we take a trip?" the teen asked, searching for ideas.

"Because the problems will still be here when we return," Alice pointed out. The teen was starting to think like her. She'd considered that very thing herself. *And we don't want him to think we're running,* she mentally added.

"And I need my medical treatment," Kathy reminded her daughter softly.

Alice and Emily looked up at Kathy, who looked almost skeletal with the skin stretched over her frame. Oddly, she also looked bloated, but they knew that was from the drugs she was taking. The bald spots looked especially bad with her bed head hair.

"Do you think you can sleep now?" Alice asked Emily, hoping her explanation of what happened hadn't made things worse for the teen. She couldn't have therapy, but Alice didn't know how to explain that without telling the teen one more thing she couldn't tell people. It was becoming ridiculous.

"Maybe," the teen told her placatingly. She had a lot to think about: everything that had happened; what Iggy had threatened her with; what Iggy had done; what her mother had done; and how she herself had blown up that house. She wasn't going to be able to sleep. "I'll try," she lied for both their sakes.

Alice knew it was a fib but was willing to give the teen her space. It was a lot to absorb, and she smiled as she tucked her daughter in bed, kissing her on the forehead. "I'm here if you have any questions," she promised. She got up with a pat on the teen's shoulder, noticing her wince. "Did you take some aspirin before you went to sleep?"

Emily nodded, wondering if it had done anything. She was still rather sore.

Kathy sat down to give Emily a kiss too. "We're both here, if you need us," she added.

"I know, Mom," Emily said sadly, seeing how ill Kathy looked and wondering how long she would be there for them. She wasn't stupid. Kathy looked horrible and was probably dying.

"Good night, darling," Kathy said as she got up and joined Alice at the door.

"Light on or off?" Alice asked.

"On," the teen said with a grimace.

Alice closed the door for privacy, and they walked back to their room.

"What did that man say to her?" Kathy demanded as soon as their bedroom door closed.

Seeing the look on her wife's face, Alice sighed but didn't hesitate to tell her. "He said he knew she was a virgin, that she *smelled* like a virgin," Alice told her. "Remember when you first got your period or the first few times you found 'come' in your underwear, and you realized you might have body odor from it?" At Kathy's confused nod, she continued, "He was playing on that and tormenting her with it. He told her he'd take her virginity from her, teach her to give head like a proper whore, and then she'd beg him to take her like a dog. He said he'd teach her to love anal, and then, he and two of his buddies would take her all at the same time. He told her they'd teach her to be their sex slave, and when they were done, they'd make money off the videos by selling them to men who love a good gangbang." She stopped, shuddering in disgust at the visual this man had given their poor daughter. "He was touching her and squeezing her breasts when he whispered all this filth in her ear. That's the kind of porn he was watching when I cut him, gangbangs."

"Good!" Kathy insisted, incensed by what Alice had told her. "He deserved it for filling her head with such filth! I hope he rots in hell! If you hadn't already killed him, I would kill him now!" she ranted, pacing about the master bedroom. "How dare he!"

"He was the one that threatened to sell her," Alice reminded her, surprised and strangely aroused at the tigress that was her angry wife. It

was very inappropriate right now with Kathy as weak as she was, but Alice recognized that and stifled those feelings.

"How did you hear him? I couldn't..."

"You were busy with your own antagonist, but I was concentrating on what that bastard was saying to her, and despite my headache, I heard him, and what I couldn't hear, I read."

Realizing that Alice could still surprise her, she nodded. "What are you going to do about Artum?" Kathy suddenly asked, realizing he was the real threat to them. He gave the orders, and he had the money to pay these disgusting and dangerous men.

"I've begun to drain his bank accounts. I set the programs up while you were showering and after I'd started dinner," Alice confided. "I've already given some of his routes away, and the Mexican cartels won't be giving those back as they encroach farther and farther into his territories."

"How are you going to stop them?" Kathy asked, suddenly afraid that Alice was getting involved with those sort of people so close to home.

Alice didn't answer that question, deliberately deflecting. "Sandi Pasternack was at that house. She might have been behind that two-way glass," Alice told her wife, watching her become furious as she realized the implications.

"That bitch! How dare she!"

"I'm setting her up too, believe me," Alice told her wife, wanting to calm her as she saw how exhausted the anger was making the sick woman. "You have a doctor's appointment in the morning. You need to sleep."

"How can I sleep now that I know all this?" Kathy asked, enraged.

"Maybe I shouldn't have told you," Alice mused aloud.

"I needed to know, Alice. Don't you dare keep me out of the loop," she threatened, pointing a finger at her wife.

"I know, baby. I know," Alice said, taking her wife in her arms as Kathy struggled weakly. "I won't."

"You know that isn't the end with Emily, don't you? We're going to have to do something."

"I'll think on it," Alice told her. She knew that Em was going to need help. Psychological help at least, and she certainly wasn't qualified to help her there.

"What if Artum comes here again?" Kathy fretted, surprised when Alice kissed her hard and passionately. By the time Alice stopped, Kathy was out of breath and strangely aroused.

"Now, you need to think about something else," Alice told her quietly, not willing to slap the hysteria out of her as she kissed her repeatedly. "I know you may not be up to this but–"

"Don't you dare stop," Kathy threatened, pulling her weakly closer and wrapping her body around Alice's. She was relishing in the curves that had grown back from Alice's own emaciated state. The muscles that had come back were wonderful to feel under her fingertips and were exciting her.

Alice kept her mind strangely detached as she made love to her wife, noting the body that was losing much of the excess flesh she'd enjoyed over the years.

Nearly half an hour later, they were both satisfied—after a fashion—and exhausted. Kathy was gently snoring in Alice's sweaty arms. Alice thought about what she had just done, using sex to distract her poor wife, but she didn't regret it. What she regretted were the muscles she had used. She ached horribly. She gently tucked Kathy into bed, covering her naked body as she slipped into the bathroom to wash herself up and take some ibuprofen. The day was going to be hell with the lack of sleep, but at least

Kathy was asleep, and she hoped Emily had managed to get some sleep with all the thoughts swirling around in her young head.

* * * * *

"We would need to know that Alice Weaver and all members of her family were out of the house for at least two hours."

"What about the housekeeper?"

"We would need the house completely clear, even the gardeners."

"That's rare. There seems to be someone around at all times." This comment proved that the house was under surveillance.

"It's those computers we need to get hold of. The history on them must be amazing."

"Remember when they confiscated the computers before? They found bupkis," someone reminded the team.

"That's because those were decoys. You don't think Alice Weaver would actually leave any incriminating evidence for us to find?"

"So, she deletes her history. Isn't there a way to retrieve stuff even if she erases it?"

"No, she does more than erase her history. She has programs that go much deeper than that, highly sophisticated programs. She encrypts her computers too, so just getting into them is impossible."

"Surely someone in our organization can get into them?"

"Yeah, we had our top people take a crack at her computers. That's how we know there is bupkis."

"They actually got a program that laughed at their efforts."

"What you mean it laughed at their efforts?"

"It was programmed with a computer-generated laugh track. was very annoying, and the laughter kept on and on. We had to pull the plug to get it to stop."

Several people chuckled at the story.

"Back to the bugging of her home. Can we get legal cause?"

"She's an international terrorist," someone asserted.

"That's unproven," someone else put in for clarity.

"She gave us information on Russian operatives, the mafia, even Kazakhstan."

"That doesn't make her an international terrorist."

"There is a treasure trove of classified information that she gave us, and how did she really get it?"

The debates were endless, and Madelyn was sick of it. Joint meetings had resumed between the FBI and the CIA, and they were fruitless. The discussions went on and on as they tried to think of ways to get probable cause, something a judge would sign off on, so they could bug Alice and Kathy Weaver's home again. Somehow, the bugs they had placed there in the past had all gone dead. The teams involved repeated their efforts, told the same stories, and came up with nothing. It was an endless loop, and people were becoming frustrated. Madelyn knew it was just a matter of time before she was pulled from this detail. The CIA didn't have anything to do with this kind of domestic research gathering. The only reason she was still involved was the American weapons found in Kazakhstan and the Russian mafia involvement. Eventually, it would be left to the FBI to watch Alice Weaver and try to charge her with something...*anything*. Madelyn had to wonder though...What was with the confiscation, and who was behind it?

Dr. Wilkerson took Alice aside before she could rejoin Kathy, who was getting pumped full of the drugs he had prescribed. Alice had stepped into the hall for a moment to take a phone call.

"Alice, do you have a minute?" Dr. Wilkerson asked as he saw her heading back to the room.

"Yeah, Doc. How's it going?" Alice asked distractedly as she put the phone back in her pocket and looked at him hopefully.

He shook his head slightly, pulling her away from the open room and out of Kathy's earshot. "That vial you gave me. How did you obtain it?"

"Why? What's in it?" Alice was suddenly very alert, her body tensed for whatever information the doctor had for her.

"That's just it, the contents have been forbidden in this country for decades," he said nervously, adjusting his glasses. Alice's intense look was making him nervous.

"Forbidden?" she asked, lifting a brow.

"Outlawed. The contents are a known carcinogen and contain some other highly questionable additives. We're reverse engineering it now, and I'm pretty certain it may be the cause of the effects we are seeing in Kathy's body." He nodded towards the room where even now the IV was dripping into the woman's arm.

"So, this substance might be the cause?" Alice clarified musingly, working to keep her anger in check as the doctor confirmed what she had already surmised.

"I don't want to say definitively it is the cause, but I'm starting to think it may be the culprit based on our tests. There was also microscopic residue of the same substance on that ring. Someone tried to wash it off,

but they weren't as thorough as they thought they were. I have several people working on it, of course."

"All are sworn to secrecy?" she suddenly worried. Her multi-tasking brain filing the comment about the ring in its proper spot. She'd get angry about that later.

"Of course," he replied indignantly.

Alice waved her hand to show she meant no harm. "Just checking. Can you cure what it caused?" Her thumb pointed back at the room where Kathy lay.

He hesitated. "It's moving rather rapidly…" he began, but at her look he added, "I can only try. That's an experimental treatment, and while I know you got her in here fast, it's moving fast too."

Alice sighed and patted him on the shoulder, surprising them both at the touch. "I know you'll do your best." She looked around and then added, "She's getting so weak, and the bloating is upsetting her."

"I'm concerned at the bruising I see on her face and–"

Alice had forgotten about the slaps her wife had received, and who knew what else had happened while Alice was unconscious. Alice still had a mild headache from the slug she'd received. She'd covered up the bruising again with carefully applied concealer. She'd offered to do the same for Kathy and Emily again today, but the teen had opted to stay home instead. She nodded, "Yeah, she fell before I could do anything…" she began, realizing how lame that sounded but offering no other excuse. She didn't want the doctor suspecting she beat her wife and suddenly realized how perpetrators of that crime got away with it using just these kind of lame lies.

He nodded. "She must be extra careful. If you need a nurse…."

Alice almost flinched at that suggestion, thinking about Sandi Pasternack and her nursing skills. Her agile mind was focused on that woman in another area. She intended to get to the bottom of that situation and take revenge on the woman. "Thank you. For now, she's comfortable at home most of the time."

He nodded. "I'll let you know if the numbers get any better. Now, let's go see our patient, eh?" He smiled optimistically and led her back to the room where Kathy was receiving treatment.

"You know, I don't know how long I can continue to do that," Kathy said as they drove away from the facility later.

"Why do you say that?" Alice asked, worrying that Kathy was giving up.

"I think that nurse stuck me three times before she found a vein, and even then, she had to dig to find it." Kathy's veins were collapsing from the meds they were pumping into her body every few days.

"They did offer to put in a port," Alice pointed out. "They still could still…."

Kathy dismissed that statement with, "And I still don't want one."

"I know, babe. I know." She reached over to pat her wife's fragile hand. "Do you want Carl's Jr. today or Wendy's?" This had become their ritual.

"I'm craving Arby's actually. You know, they have that orange shake with cream? Reminds me of a Creamsicle."

"Arby's it is then," Alice smiled indulgently as she laughed.

They enjoyed these little 'picnics' as Alice called them, even if Kathy would throw up the food later. Heading home, Kathy said, "I want to shave off the remaining hair on my head. Will you stop at Mervyn's, so I can pick up a hat or scarf?"

Alice looked at her wife. The thick, luxurious, brown hair was so thin and straggly now that it looked greasy. The bald patches were evident all over, and she could see why Kathy wanted the hair gone. "You don't want a wig?" she asked instead.

"No, that would probably fall off and embarrass me. I'm going for a look," she teased her wife and smiled.

Alice nodded as she headed to the mall and the nearest Mervyn's. Alice didn't want to shop throughout the mall, her own aching body objecting at the walk around the store. They shopped for only a little while, picking out a straw hat that seemed summery and festive. Kathy also found two silk scarves that she liked, one red and one black. Alice smiled at these simple pleasures, hoping Kathy's ill health was only a temporary thing as she paid for her wife's purchases.

"Will you shave my head?" Kathy asked when they were home again.

"Are you sure?"

Kathy nodded and led her wife into their bathroom.

Alice fetched the scissors that Kathy had kept for crafting projects with the kids. They were heavy steel scissors and super sharp. She had Kathy sit on the toilet and lean forward as she snipped the remaining long, straggly strands from her scalp and dropped them into a wastepaper bin. When she was done, Kathy looked up and the women exchanged a look in the mirror. She looked horrible, and the cuts were choppy and uneven. Kathy reached into the shower for a razor and handed it to Alice. Gulping slightly, Alice reached for the shower wand. "Bend over a little," she told Kathy as she dampened the remaining hair on her close-cropped head. Once everything was wet, she took the shaving gel in her hand and rubbed it all over Kathy's scalp. Gently, she began to scrape the razor over her wife's head. Long, sure strokes took the short hairs away, and short, rapid

strokes removed the stubble. Finally, Kathy's scalp was smooth and hairless. Alice rinsed off the last of the foaming gel, wiping her wife's head with a fluffy towel as she watched the suds go down the drain in the middle of the shower floor. She gulped as Kathy looked up, her bald head gleaming in the light of the bathroom. "Well, how do you like it?" Alice asked cheerfully.

Kathy looked at herself. "Well, it's better than it was," she said optimistically, but she could see that she didn't look good bald. Her head looked an odd shape to her. It was a shock. She felt the cold immediately, despite the heat of the summer day. "I don't think I would want to go out in public like this," she admitted, then laughed as she helped Alice clean up. A wave of nausea hit her, and she was forced to sit back while Alice finished up. "I did ask for it though," she admitted as she stared at herself in the mirror.

"Fortunately, it will grow back," Alice tried to console her. She didn't tell her wife how bad she looked; she would keep that tidbit to herself. Kathy's sallow skin and the taut look as her skin stretched over her bones were magnified by the bruising that was always faintly present. The bloated look from some of the pills she was taking completed the look, and it all made her look horrible.

"I'm going to scare the kids," she said with a smile.

"They know what's going on."

"I'm glad they aren't younger. This is scary," she answered, turning her head to and fro as she looked at the effects of her baldness.

"Maybe we should have waited for Halloween?"

Kathy laughed and got up, brushing stray hairs from her collar. Unbuttoning her shirt, she went to change into another. Tying a scarf

around her now cold head, she looked at herself in the mirror, determining that the scarf looked stylish.

"Why red?" Alice asked, watching her as she tossed the towels into the hamper with the shirt Kathy had discarded.

"I'll wear the black one tomorrow."

The kids were startled. Sean blurted, "Now, you really do look sick," before he put his hand to his mouth and said, "Sorry."

"No, you're right. I do," Kathy admitted, letting him off the hook and giving him a hug. "But I'm still here, and now, I'll save on shampoo."

He laughed as she had intended, but it was a hollow laugh. The kids couldn't help looking at her repeatedly through dinner as they attempted to make conversation.

"When is your next appointment?" Emily asked.

"Day after tomorrow. Why?"

"I thought I'd come along. Maybe I could get a new tennis racket?"

"You got a new tennis racket when you started lessons this summer," Alice pointed out, her eyes narrowing.

"I accidentally hit the edge and busted it," the teen admitted.

"Emily, I'm not made of money," Alice said exasperatedly. "You have got to learn to take care of your things."

"I hate to tell you," Sean said, bringing his parents attention to himself, "but I'm going to need new football cleats and a few other things."

Alice sighed, but deep down, she relished these common, everyday things. They were such a welcome relief from the more complicated things she had on her plate.

After they cleaned up the kitchen and the kids had gone off to watch television or play video games, Alice just held Kathy as they watched the sun set.

"What do you have planned?" Kathy asked, glancing at the ever-present gardeners, who even now were patrolling the fence line and planting some weird, fast-growing trees that wouldn't grow too tall and obscure their line of sight but would offer better privacy. They were working late. Given what she now knew, she realized they were probably here to defend the family against Artum or whoever else was out there.

"I've redirected most of Artum's money that I could find in Richard's books. I've also made Sandi penniless and put red flags on her credit, so she may lose her house sooner rather than later."

"What good will that do?" Kathy asked bitterly, gesturing to the bruise on her arm from the IV earlier.

"That will make her desperate and more amenable to other plans I have for her."

"Can you tell me what you have in mind?"

"My plans are not concrete yet, and I don't want to burden you..." she began, then seeing her wife's mutinous look, she glanced around to make sure they weren't being overheard. The bench they were sitting on overlooked the Pacific Ocean and was far from anyone walking on the path. In fact, they were alone. She began to tell her wife her plan, and Kathy's eyes opened wide as she realized how diabolical Alice's mind really was. Remembering what the doctor had told her about the ring, Alice's multi-tasking mind was thinking of other things she could do to Sandi beyond what she was telling her wife as she kept her temper carefully under control.

"Do you think it will work?" Kathy asked excitedly.

Alice shrugged her elegant little shoulders. "I don't know," she admitted honestly. "A lot of things will have to fall into place, and I don't

want to get my hopes up. That's why I really didn't want to tell you; I didn't want to jinx the plan."

Kathy laughed at the superstition she could hear in her wife's admission. "I'm certain you can make it happen with just a few minor adjustments."

Alice looked around and stiffened slightly. "I think it's time we made our way back to the house."

Kathy looked around and saw two men at the end of the path. They were far from their house, but these men were out of place in this area and were not dressed for a walk by the ocean. She nodded and slowly got up as they casually walked back to their estate and unlocked the gate, being careful to relock it behind them as they went in. "Do you think that was Artum or his men?" Kathy asked fearfully.

"I'm certain it was them," Alice admitted and made a jerking motion with her head to one of the gardeners, pointing back where they had come from. The man nodded and put down his shovel, nudging another man to join him as they went to check out whatever it was that Alice had seen.

"Will this ever end?" Kathy wondered as they walked across the lawn. They were admiring their beautiful house, which gave them a feeling of contentment just seeing it and knowing it was their home for all these years. She didn't want to lose those feelings or the house.

"I'm hoping to bring everything to an end," Alice told her earnestly, worrying that there was too much stress for her wife. "I want it *all* to end."

* * * * *

They enjoyed a couple days of family time. Alice took both kids to get the gear they needed, and then, Kathy had her appointment. Emily opted to stay home again, chatting on the phone with a friend from school just like the old days. Both her mothers were relieved that she was able to find some sort of normalcy amidst the chaos that was their secret life. Sean had asked and received permission to go to Geoff's house for the night for a marathon session of video games with three other guys. Alice had supplied him with a big box of snacks and sodas, so Geoff's parents wouldn't be overwhelmed by the boy's appetite. As she gave him the keys to the Rav4, she cautioned him, "No drinking."

"Naw, I don't like the taste," he admitted. "The soda will be fine."

Alice smiled, not fooled. He had just admitted that he had drunk alcohol, and she'd follow up on that another time. She didn't want to ruin this evening.

"Let's go," Kathy said tiredly as she got into the Rover with Alice, and they headed to the clinic.

The sessions had become repetitive. One session in the week was one set of drugs, the other session another set. The deadly cocktail was showing no signs of being effective, and this was worrying Alice. Dr. Wilkerson seemed startled to see a now bald Kathy but hid his expression well as he greeted her and had the nurse insert her IV.

"I'm going to adjust Kathy's meds now that we know more about this," he indicated the chart he was showing Alice on the vial she had brought him, confirming the source of Kathy's disease.

Alice nodded in agreement, not even thinking about telling her wife of the change. She didn't need additional things to worry about.

"You know, I don't want to go to any of the fast-food places," Kathy admitted. "Throwing up that greasy food later hurts."

"Would you like a better quality vomit offering?" Alice suggested, and they both laughed.

"No, I have soup and crackers waiting at the house, and that's enough for me. I just want to get home and crawl into bed today."

"Are you feeling worse than usual?" Alice asked worriedly.

"No, I'm just tired and want to go home. Maybe a hot bath and crackers will make me feel better?"

Alice obliged her wife, taking Kathy directly home and offering her inane conversation that had them both chuckling. She delighted in thinking of things to make her wife laugh and smile.

Alice was so focused on caring for Kathy, she missed that none of the gardeners were about as she parked the Rover in the garage. Helping her wife slowly climb the steps into the house, she also didn't feel the ominous presence in her home. But when she saw Emily tied to a dining room chair in the middle of the living room, she froze, her hand on Kathy's arm tightening reflexively.

"Hello, Alice," Artum drawled as he gestured towards the two women. "Please, come in and be seated," he offered hospitably.

Alice was only startled for a moment. She realized now that she hadn't seen the gardeners on her drive up the driveway, which could mean only one thing: they were dead or had been removed. She assessed the room. The teen looked frightened but had a maddened glaze in her eyes, making them look an odd shade of green, and the gag in Emily's mouth prevented her from voicing her concerns to her mother. Alice saw Artum standing there looking victorious. Next to him was one of his goons and strangely, a third person that was a dwarf. Artum looked pompous, sporting his goatee and standing with his arms crossed. He was leaning on one leg, the other slightly bent in a cocky stance.

Alice didn't take Artum up on his generous offer of a seat. She gently pushed Kathy towards the couch as though they were obeying him, then she quickly turned and ran at him. Using his slightly bent knee to launch herself, she stepped up on his hip with her foot and took a leap over the length of his torso to his shoulder and kicked him in the head. He was unused to supporting that much weight, and the unexpected blow caused him to bend over. Alice allowed herself to jump down, then putting all her weight into her elbow, she smashed his cranium on her way down, knocking him out as they both fell to the ground.

"Son of a bitch!" she swore, wishing she could rub her now sore elbow. She was out of breath and slow to get up. She realized it had been a long time since she trained.

The second man, expecting conversation and startled by her attack, took a swing at Alice. She leaned back slightly, letting his punch go by her. Her arm then wrapped around his arm, pulling it at an unnatural angle, and they both heard the sickening crunch as she broke his arm. Releasing the arm, she brought the heel of her hand up and crunched into his nose, pushing the cartilage back into his brain. She briefly thought, *This is becoming a habit*, as she pulled back, and he dropped to the floor, blood oozing from his nostrils.

The small man leapt onto Alice's back, thwarting her attempts to reach him with her lethal hands or feet. He clung on like a spider, and Alice could feel him attempting to wrap his hands around her throat. She twisted and turned, trying to dislodge him. Suddenly, she did a neat little flip forward and landed on her back where he was lodged. The blow knocked the air out of his lungs as her small body landed on his even smaller one. Alice made sure her elbow struck his solar plexus, and he gasped, trying to get oxygen into his lungs. Alice didn't give him the chance, striking

repeatedly with her elbow. He had exhaled but couldn't draw in any air, and his face turned red then blue from the lack of oxygen. His hands grasped at his throat, then he reached towards his attacker in a plea for mercy. Alice pounded again and again and only stopped when his body went completely limp.

Crawling over to his prone body, she fished around and found a pocketknife in his front pocket. He sighed as his body relaxed and farted loudly. She wrinkled her nose distastefully as she found the knife, pulled it open, and slit his throat. She used the spurting blood and his handkerchief to rub her fingerprints from the handle.

Alice felt a blow to her head as Artum came to and attacked. She rolled with it. "You hit like a girl," Alice gasped, wanting to rub the sore spot, but there was no time. She rolled again to give her room to get away from the crazed man, who got in several well-aimed blows. He tried to stomp on her, but she rolled again, and then, reversing herself, she grabbed at the foot that was attempting to stomp her again. She struck at the back of his leg, unbalancing him, and he crashed to the floor. Alice wasn't about to let him get up again. She used her sore elbow on him, like what she had done to the small man.

"You…won't…succeed…" Artum gasped, his hands closing on Alice's neck as he tried to choke her.

She used her arms to try to break his grip. He was a strong man with a longer reach, and she was so much smaller. She saw stars when he squeezed her throat. She knew she didn't have a lot of time to do anything fancy. She was in a prone position, at a disadvantage, and unable to get leverage. She swung her head forward, using her forehead to butt against his chin twice. Her head hurt dreadfully. It was still recovering from earlier that week, and now, it was being used as a battering ram.

Fortunately, it was effective. Artum loosened his grip marginally, and that was all Alice needed. Her arms broke his arms apart, and she rolled into a crouching position, ready to attack as the man got up. He was still bleeding from his lip where her forehead had smashed it against his teeth, and his jaw hurt from her attack. As he began to rise, was still unbalanced, Alice attacked. Her knee struck him in the eye, his head swung back, and he fell to the floor. Reaching in his jacket, he pulled out a gun and called her, "Schlyukha!" a whore in Russian.

Alice laughed as she responded in Russian and told him what she really thought of him. His eyes widened as he realized she not only understood what he had said but spoke the language. While she did not speak perfectly, it was adequate to make herself understood. He began to rise again; certain he had the upper hand now with the gun. Alice slowly approached him; her hands raised in surrender. Emily and Kathy looked on, horrified that Alice was going to be shot. As she got closer to Artum, Alice continued her insults of him in Russian, then she slapped the gun aside, painfully aware of her wife and daughter's location in the room, ensuring the gun wouldn't fire into either of them. She grabbed it from his hand and twisted that same hand to the point that it nearly broke his wrist. Using sleight of hand, she twisted the gun around, holding it steadily on him.

"What are you going to do now, whore?" he sneered, breathing hard at their exertions. He was shocked and surprised at how fast the woman had moved; that had been totally unexpected. Maybe there had been some truth in the stories Sebastian had told him. He had doubted so much of what he said and attributed it to the old man's admiration for the pretty woman.

"Kill you," she told him, focusing on him and pulling the trigger without hesitation. The thunderous roar of the gun was loud in the house, and she kept pulling the trigger until it clicked on an empty chamber. The first shots had taken Sebastian down, and Alice directed the remaining bullets to his heart, liver, and then, his head, continuing to fire deliberately and effectively. He was dead after the third bullet, but still she kept shooting, taking her frustrations out on his dead body.

"Alice. ALICE!" Kathy called, trying to get her to stop. Surely the shots would bring the police to their quiet little neighborhood.

Alice looked up, startled to see her wife and daughter in the room. The bloodlust was high in her, and she sagged in defeat as she dropped the gun and went to untie Emily. Kathy sank gratefully onto the couch, exhausted from her medical treatment and relieved that her wife was still alive.

"Go get those firecrackers and other fireworks I gave you and Sean for the Fourth of July. Hurry!" Alice told Emily to distract the dazed teen after she untied her.

"What?"

"We need to light them off now. HURRY!"

Emily suddenly heard her mother's words clearly and ran to get them. She was shaking so hard she fumbled and scattered them in her room. Alice was waiting at the bottom of the steps and took several from Emily as she returned. They went out on the steps and started lighting them off. One was a bottle rocket and soared into the air, whistling and whining until it went out with a pop. Alice hoped the distraction was enough to annoy the neighbors and allay any fears they might have had about gunshots. She slowly returned to the house with the teen after they lit several more fireworks over the course of about five minutes.

"If anyone asks, we are celebrating a milestone in your Mom's treatment."

"Are we?"

"No," Alice said sadly, shaking her head at the teen.

* * * * *

"Crap!" Kathy said, running her fingers along her bald pate.

"What? Did I miss something?" Alice asked, looking around and then up at her wife.

"He's bleeding," she gestured to where the men lay on the rug where Alice had downed them.

"Yeah...so?" Alice asked, confused and trying to see what was bothering Kathy.

"That's a real Persian rug. It'll cost a fortune to replace."

Alice looked to see if Kathy was sincere and started laughing. It took her several moments to catch her breath, and Kathy joined in after watching her wife lose her normally masterful control. Emily looked on in consternation, not getting the joke at all. Finally, Alice wound down and wiped the tears from her eyes. "You realize we are going to have to burn that?" she pointed at the bloodstained carpet.

Kathy nodded, wiping her eyes on the sleeves of her shirt, then grabbing a tissue from the box on an end table and blowing her nose. "Just make sure you get all the ashes ground up."

"And composted," Alice agreed.

"Wait. What is going on?" Emily asked, completely confused about why her mothers had been laughing.

Alice looked at her daughter sadly. "This is about getting rid of this," she gestured to the room at large.

"Mom, you aren't going to report this, right?" the teen confirmed, perhaps more frightened than when the men had grabbed her and tied her up. She'd been on the computer, then suddenly, they'd appeared in her room. She hadn't heard them enter the house at all. Her music had been turned up loud with her mothers gone, and she hadn't thought to activate the alarm system, feeling complacent in their family home and used to the security that Alice offered them when she was around.

Alice shook her head, completely sober. She glanced at Kathy, then again at Emily, debating what to say to her.

"They'd throw away the key if they found out, wouldn't they?"

Alice nodded, waiting to see how Emily would react. She wondered what her daughter would say in the aftermath of this violence. She looked...dazed...confused...and frightened, as she should.

"You can't confess!" the teen suddenly blurted.

Alice shook her head, her eyes still their odd shade of orange, and she waited.

"This is justifiable homicide, Mom; you can prove that." Emily sounded almost as though she were pleading with Alice to hear her.

Kathy looked on, seeing the odd look in her daughter's eyes, and her heart was breaking slightly.

"Mom, I never want anything like this to happen again," she continued, sounding hysterical. "I don't want any of those..." she searched for the correct word, "thugs to touch me again!" She shuddered as she remembered how helpless she had felt when they asked her where her parents were, then tied her up and gagged her. She looked up at Kathy and saw how helpless her mother looked, and then, she looked at Alice

standing there looking healthy. She had certainly kicked ass and that, above all, had made an impression on the young woman's psyche. "You have to teach me, Mom. I can't ever again let people like that," she gestured again, looking almost desperate, "get away with what they did. They were going to kill us all. They were determined to kill you." She waited for Alice to say something, and when she didn't, Emily added, "I won't tell anyone. Honest. But you've got to teach me to defend myself. You've *got* to teach me to cope…with this," she said hysterically, gesturing at the carnage in their living room.

"This isn't about me. This is about you and what you are willing to accept into your life. I am not a saint. I never claimed to be. And I don't want this," Alice gestured to herself and the first body on the ground, "for you…*ever*."

"Don't you see, Mom? I am in *this*," she returned defiantly, not afraid of Alice. She knew her mother loved her, would never hurt her, and would *die* for her. "I may be young, but I get that you are trying to protect me, and I understand you didn't ever want me to know about all *this*. But maybe I was meant to find out. Maybe, of all your children, I was meant to learn from you and right the wrongs." She saw the startled look in Alice's eyes. She didn't back away from the cat-like narrowing of her pupils or the fading orange tint she could still see in the iris. "I know you aren't a killer. I know you have compassion and reason and whatever it takes to defend yourself. Don't you think I deserve to know how to do that to the best of my ability?"

"I don't want you seeking out this…crap," Alice finished lamely. "I don't want this for you," she repeated, sounding devastated for her daughter, feeling helpless not knowing exactly how to help her.

"I don't want it either," the teen put in. "I stumbled across it, and maybe the fates wanted me to find out about you. Maybe these things," she gestured at the cooling bodies at their feet, "simply find certain people. Don't you think I deserve to know how to defend myself from situations not of my own making?"

Kathy was startled, and the reasoning of her teenaged daughter choked her up. It was obvious that Emily had been thinking this out. Kathy exchanged a look with Alice and surprised them both by croaking, "Teach her."

Alice stared at her wife hard. She was incredulous to hear her saying that. "Kathy, no...We agreed...."

Kathy shook her head and made a negative gesture with hand. "That was before. She's right. Things have a way of finding us. She needs to be protected, and Sean needs protection. We can't be there for them all the time. They're getting older. They'll be going out into the world, and they need to know how to protect themselves."

"You want me to confess to Sean what I am?" Alice asked, shocked and alarmed. She stared at Kathy, wondering if her meds were affecting her brain. Seeing the bald woman before her holding the straw hat and scarf in her hands that usually hid her now bare skin, Kathy looked almost alien to Alice.

"No, I don't want you to confess to Sean, but maybe he could use some combat skills. You know, maybe learn some defensive moves for life and for grace," she shrugged her shoulders, showing how thin she was becoming from the drugs being pumped into her body every week. Her face was round and swelling up, and it looked terrible with the taut skin in certain areas making it appear misshapen. The bones of her shoulder and collarbone were peeking through the shirt. "Maybe he might have need of

those skills? I just know he needs to be home more and bonding with you before he's off to college next year. He needs to know you, Alice."

"Don't talk like you aren't going to be here," Alice demanded, determined to make Kathy see that this was not a good plan of action. "You're going to make it. Doctor–"

"Doesn't know if I will make it either," Kathy finished for her. "All we can do is try. All we can do is prepare our children the best ways we know how." She glanced at Emily listening to them, her heart breaking for her youngest daughter…her last child…her baby. "I'm sorry you didn't get a chance to keep your childhood a bit longer."

"Mom, that wasn't your doing," Emily told her, sounding older than her years. She put a hand on her mother's arm and gently squeezed. Kathy noted that Emily's hand was slightly shaking, and she was relieved that the child wasn't becoming cold-blooded about all this. "I think Carmen started that. It wasn't your fault that I overheard and saw what I did."

"I should have been a better mother," Kathy lamented, watching the last of Emily's childhood burn up before her. It was in the ether sphere, but she could feel it; it was almost tangible.

"You *are* a good mother," the teen insisted. She looked back at Alice. "What are we going to do with these?" she asked, glancing at the bodies.

"*We* aren't going to do anything," Alice told her automatically. "I'll–"

"No, Alice. She needs to know," Kathy interrupted, "the good, the bad, and the ugly."

Alice stared incredulously at what her wife was saying. "No, Kathy. She doesn't need to know."

"Yes, Alice. She might have need of that knowledge…someday."

"Your meds are addling your mind," she said aloud.

Kathy smiled, looking more like a Halloween decoration as her teeth showed prominently in her pale face, almost like horse teeth. "Probably, but then I think you addled my mind a long time ago," she teased. "Teach her," she repeated meaningfully. "Teach her to defend herself. Give her the confidence to go out in the world and not be afraid of such ugliness," her hands gestured at the bodies, one of which released a stream of gas in a long, drawn out hiss. "Teach her the good too?" she pleaded hopefully, almost crying at what she was asking Alice to do.

"No," Alice said, shaking her head, "I won't!"

"For me?" Kathy asked, hating herself for using her illness like this, but she was afraid of the madness she had seen in the teen's eyes. Emily had seen too much and experienced too much death and destruction at such a young age, and she had no outlet for it. The child couldn't see a therapist without sending her parents to jail, and neither parent was qualified to give her psychiatric care. There had to be an outlet, and the only thing Kathy could think of was having Alice teach her to stay out of trouble…the only way Alice knew how.

Alice sighed, wanting to cry as Kathy pleaded with her. "I'll teach her," she agreed.

* * * * *

They had to wait until dark, and in the meantime, Alice grabbed some plastic painting cloths from the garage. She rolled the bodies with Emily's reluctant help. It was obvious the teen was forcing herself, and despite Alice's initial reluctance to allow the teen to participate, she let her work through it. She could see by the way Emily handled the bodies that she was angry at them for forcing her to do this. Not angry at Alice or Kathy

but at the men Alice had killed. It was their fault she had to help clean up their bodies.

Alice showed Emily how to clean the gun and put the men's fingerprints on the gun by repeatedly placing it in their grips. Using her own gloved hand to handle the gun, she pocketed it in the first man's pocket before rolling him up. The dwarf confused her, and she was surprised when she found his passport on his body. She stripped that from his body along with the large roll of American dollars she found.

"Shopping," Emily murmured, trying some humor.

"Charity," Alice swiftly retaliated, then softened her voice when the teen looked upset. "We don't need any of this money."

"I know," she said softly, helping to check the dead men's pockets before rolling them in the plastic sheets.

Kathy was unable to help; she had barely any strength left. One by one, Alice and Emily pulled, dragged, and pushed the bodies through the house and down the steps to the back of the Rover. In the garage, they were able to use a wheelbarrow to get the bodies into the vehicle. Stacking them in there, Alice had never been so glad about the size of their enclosed garage. She returned after they took the surprisingly heavy little man out to the Rover and found Kathy attempting to roll up their expensive Persian rug.

"I'll do that. Why don't you get a fire going in the fire pit? We'll have a barbecue, and later, we'll burn this."

Kathy nodded, exhausted. As she got up, she lost her balance slightly and nearly fell. She tried to hide it, but Alice saw and got up to support her. Taking a moment to give her wife a hug, she reassured her, "I'll take care of it." Alice could feel Kathy's bones against her during the hug. Kathy nodded, a little sob escaping her throat.

"I know you will." She went out and painfully put wood in the pit and threw the grate over the fire.

It was well after dark as they fed pieces of the rug into the fire. They'd cooked hamburgers on the grill, and Emily had been amazed that she'd been able to eat. The rug smelled funny, but they took their time and burned it slowly. Alice had cut the carpet into convenient squares, and her hand was hurting from using the knife so long. The rug had proved resilient to her attempts to cut it, and the bruise in the palm of her hand added to the large inventory of cuts and bruises she now sported on her body. She'd been on the phone a couple times during the evening, and Kathy quietly asked her about it.

"The gardeners were pulled off the job. Artum had set up a distraction with his men, and they'd gone to deal with it. I'm glad they aren't dead, but I gave them hell for leaving us unprotected."

"Why don't you let them deal with...?" Kathy gestured towards the house where Alice had Emily spritzing bleach and a combination of other chemicals to make the house smell clean and fresh. Mrs. Fernandez would return from her days off to a sparkling, fresh house. "Bleach would be a dead giveaway," Alice had explained to Emily, showing her the combination of cleaning supplies that would work on blood, body fluids, and DNA. She'd shown her how to clean the scene. She also showed her how well blood showed up under a blue light if they didn't clean thoroughly.

"I won't let them deal with cleaning the house because I don't want them to know Artum is gone. That wouldn't be good for business," Alice said meaningfully. This had happened so quickly. She hadn't been quite prepared, and it annoyed her. The phone calls had annoyed her as well. She'd kept them short, using a burner phone she had and afterward,

throwing the phone in the fire with the damn carpet that was taking forever. It had been a large area rug. "So, what kind of rug are you going to shop for to replace this?" Alice asked in a forced attempt to be cheerful and change the subject. She used a poker to lift the lump of plastic that used to be a phone back into the flames and further destroy it.

Kathy laughed, as she was meant to. She also yawned. Her eyes were sunk deeply in the sockets of her head, and she looked terrible.

"Why don't you go to bed, love. I'll handle this," Alice gestured to the fire. It was going to take hours to burn all this, and she could see how exhausted Kathy was already.

"*We* will take care of it, Mom," Emily corrected and neither Mom was certain who she was addressing.

Kathy smiled wanly. She wished she could do more, but she knew she couldn't. She nodded and got up to head inside. Alice rose to help her. "Don't put any more on there until that is gone," she instructed the teen, nodding to the fire where even now the rug pieces were attempting to smother the flames. She noted grimly that it was a really good rug, even as it tried to thwart their attempts to burn it thoroughly.

Alice helped Kathy get ready for bed, washing her tenderly and lovingly, then tucking her in.

"Teach her," Kathy repeatedly weakly as she grabbed Alice's hand. "I'm sorry."

"I am too, baby. I am too," Alice replied as she patted her hand. Kathy was asleep in minutes, simply exhausted.

"Why don't we use gasoline on the carpet?" Emily asked Alice when she returned to the fire with another bundle in her hands. It had been at least an hour since she left to take Kathy to bed, and the teen had started to worry.

"Because it would leave a trace, and we don't want that," she replied as she saw the carpet pile hadn't gone down as much as she had hoped. She put her bundle down next to it and began cutting up the shirts, the pants, and the other clothing she had brought.

"What is that?"

"It's the clothes those men were wearing. I stripped the bodies," Alice admitted, talking in an undertone. Sound really carried at night, and it was very dark as they fed their fire.

"Is that to help prevent them from being identified?" the teen asked, and Alice nodded as she tried not to stare into the fire—it was tempting as sitting before a fire was a time for reflection. How dare those men break into her home again?

Emily had admitted she hadn't set the alarm and had turned her music up way too loud. They had taken her because she was distracted by her friend on the phone, and the music had covered the sounds of their entry. She was ashamed and vowed to learn everything Alice could teach her.

* * * * *

It was early morning but still quite dark before the carpet and clothing were all burned up in the fire. Now, Alice had had to find something to burn besides the logs and other wood they kept for this purpose. She'd broken up some wood shelving she kept in the garage, burning the particle board instead of the treated lumber. She explained her reasoning to Emily and wondered how much of it the teen would even remember as she yawned.

"Gawd, I'm tired," the teen admitted as they stirred the ashes of the fire, making sure it was down to almost nothing.

"We aren't done," Alice reminded her, just as tired and hurting. She was out of shape and older, not used to this type of activity.

"Oh…yeah," the girl replied, wondering what they were going to do about the now naked bodies in the back of her mom's Rover.

"Grab your fishing gear and change your clothes. We are going fishing."

"What? Fishing?" the girl asked, surprised. Alice made sure the fire was nearly out. Only a few smoldering pieces of wood were left, and she used the poker to move them to the middle, so they would burn together. They could see no further signs of the clothing and carpeting they'd spent the night burning.

Alice stretched as she changed into her fishing gear. It had been a long time since she'd taken the kids fishing or been out on a boat. She tried to remember the last time and couldn't. She was so tired, but she had to do this. The bodies had been in the back of the SUV far too long already. She packed the fishing gear in the back seats, and she and Emily got in the front. It was still very dark, but she could feel the air was clear and knew it would be a glorious morning when the sun came up. The missing windows meant they were cold in the SUV, and she cranked up the heat. Alice laughed at the ever-present vehicle parked down their street and the two men asleep in the front seats.

"Why don't they give up?" Emily asked her mother.

"They have a job to do. They are probably being paid very well to watch us."

"Not doing a very good job, are they?"

Alice laughed again and drove past without worrying about being followed.

"Do you own this boat?" Emily asked in a quiet, little voice as they drove into the marina. Alice seemed to know exactly where she was going.

"No, I rented this boat. That was one of the phone calls I made," she admitted as they started carrying their gear to the boat. "Get the covers off and fold them," she told the girl, pointing to the ones she meant. She hoped that anyone watching them would see their gear and stop watching, assuming they were just going early morning fishing. It was early even for fishing, but Alice wanted no witnesses as she hoisted the body of the little person onto her shoulder. The tarp she had brought along to cover the plastic sheet was hiding him from view. Her back protested, and she anticipated Artum and the other man causing her back even more pain. Thankfully, she found a wheelbarrow unattended and temporarily confiscated it to use for the other two bodies as Emily helped her get them on board. As they were loading the last body, they froze. Just as they had lifted Artum's body, they both heard a door open and shut somewhere along the marina, the sound carrying clearly on the early morning air. Finally, when everything was clear and all three bodies were hidden on deck, Alice stole a few chunks of concrete that some other boaters were using for weights. Emily returned the wheelbarrow as Alice readied the boat she had rented.

They sailed slowly out of the harbor, their lights leading the way. Alice had dimmed the lights immediately in front of her, so they didn't blind her and prevent her seeing their passage.

"Why that harbor, Mom?" Emily asked once they were on their way and Alice was showing her how to drive the boat.

"I used to have a boat. Do you remember that?"

The teen shook her head. "Is that what made you think of this way of getting rid of the bodies? Is that what you used to do?"

Alice smiled, the gesture pulling the skin taut on her face and showing her where there were more hurts on her battered body. Artum had landed a few blows. "Yes, I did this a time or two before, and we are going to use about the same area. There is a shelf here, and then, it drops off deeply. We will tie the bodies to those cinder blocks and throw them overboard."

"Good. Can we go home and sleep after that's done?" the tired teen asked.

Alice shook her head. "No, we need fish for our cover story, so we actually have to do some fishing."

Emily sighed and decided she better stop complaining or Alice might not teach her anymore.

They were out for hours. Alice showed Emily how to tie a knot to the concrete that wasn't about to come loose. She explained that fish would eat the flesh and even the bones of the bodies.

"Are you sure they can't trace anything back to us?" the teen fretted.

"No, but you should never be too sure of that. Always assume that you've left some trace, and they will find you. Be prepared."

"How do you live with that?"

Alice shrugged. "I'm good, Emily. I'm *really* good, and most of my life I've been *really* careful."

Emily realized the way her mother had worded that last sentence. "And now?" she asked, knowingly.

Alice grimaced as they dumped the unknown man first, watching him submerge and seeing the bubbles rise as he sank. Emily watched avidly well after he was out of sight. "I think I'm just getting old, and I hope I'm not getting careless. I just want it to stop."

"Well, you're done here, right?"

Alice shook her head. "No, there will always be a need for a cleanup on aisle three," she quipped.

"Huh?"

Alice smiled. "You need to learn obscure references, Em. It means that I will have to clean this up for a while; there are still some loose ends." She didn't tell her daughter about the senator or Mrs. Pasternack. She hoped she could leave Emily out of *that* distasteful business, especially with what had happened with that twit of a daughter the woman had whelped. Her eyes glittered as she thought of Sandi and the drug that Doctor Wilkerson was reverse engineering for her.

"I do pretty well in school," the teen pointed out.

"Yes, and we're grateful that you are a straight A student. Now, I want you to take more classes."

"*More* classes? I'm maxed out."

"I mean extracurricular classes."

"Like karate?" she asked hopefully, having asked for those a few times. She felt so foolish watching herself in the mirror as she imitated the karate she had watched on YouTube or other videos she had seen.

"No, not karate yet. I'll begin to teach you some of the martial arts, but I want you to take dance classes and–"

"Dance classes!" the teen cut her off, nearly shouting in consternation.

"Shhh. Sound carries over the water, and you'll draw attention to us," Alice warned her, looking about in the darkness. The lights of their boat were turned off, but who knew what or who might be out here. She could barely see anything with the curve of the Earth. They were well offshore as they tied a block to the little person's ankles. For a dwarf, he had a big penis, and Alice looked away.

Watching the little man slip under the waves Alice tried to remember the last time she had disposed of a body in this way and realized it had been an exceptionally long time. She was glad of that and hoped this would be the last time. She was so tired of it all.

Artum was the biggest of the men, and the multiple holes in his body had leaked blood all over the plastic. It was a good thing Alice had rolled him up in the plastic again after removing his clothes as it held in all the gory mess. She'd had a hard time removing his clothes. They'd been fine clothes too, despite the many gunshot holes. She'd been surprised to find he wore women's underwear but shrugged, knowing some men found them more comfortable, and who was she to judge? She was glad when Artum slipped below the water and was gone. She poured pure bleach where the bodies had lain on the deck of the boat, washing it down with a hose as the waste poured through the drain holes on the sides of the boat deck. She poured the last of the bleach on the tarps they had used, then using the last of the blocks she had brought for this purpose, she tied them to the plastic and tarps and threw them overboard. She watched to see they were weighted down enough to go below the surface and disappear, carrying any remaining DNA with them. Lastly, she threw the gun overboard, glad to have it gone.

"Let's go fishing!" Alice said brightly to the tired and now too quiet teen.

Emily had never felt less like fishing, but she was following Alice's lead and tried to wake herself as Alice fired up the boat and headed to a likely fishing spot.

They didn't catch much; they were simply too tired. Alice's weary body was protesting as she fought the line for her own catch. Emily's was bigger, which cheered the exhausted teen. "Why dancing classes?" the

teen asked while waiting for a fish to bite the line that Alice had shown her how to tie and then, how to bait the hook.

"You are going to need poise and skills you aren't yet aware of. It will teach you the balance and grace that I can't teach you in combat fighting. It will give you all the things you don't know you need. I also want you to learn fencing, and we'll take classes together," she promised.

"You will?" the teen asked, suddenly sounding enthusiastic.

"Oh, yeah." Alice sounded pleased with the idea herself. "I want you to take languages at school too."

"Why?" the teen sounded dismayed as they brought in another fish, and Alice finally called it quits. She knew she was becoming dangerously tired and this could lead to mistakes…and mistakes were dangerous.

"Languages will teach your mind to use different pathways. Take Latin for the basics, which will help you with any of the other languages you choose. You need a well-rounded education, and I intended to speak with you about taking those anyway."

"How long do I have to study?" Emily sounded like a normal teen, whining at all the extra study and work Alice was requiring.

"The rest of your life," Alice admitted. "I only learned Russian a few years ago," she pointed out.

Emily quit whining as she thought about the things Alice wanted her to do and the reasons behind them. She didn't understand, but she knew if she asked, Alice would tell her. She just had to remember to ask the *right* questions. She didn't think Alice would mislead her, but she might not answer the questions completely if she didn't word them correctly.

* * * * *

Alice slept well into the afternoon, and Emily slept just as long.

"Is Mom sick?" Sean asked when he came home the next morning and saw she was still in bed. He looked at Kathy, wondering if she should be in bed as he watched her popping some pills.

"Naw, just a late night. You should have been here," Kathy told him brightly, secretly thinking, *Thank God you weren't here.*

"Yeah? What'd you do?"

"Your Mom grilled some hamburgers, and we made marshmallows and smores." *And she killed three men in the living room,* Kathy thought.

"Sounds good. Anything left?" he asked as he headed to the refrigerator to look for leftovers.

"No, sorry," she told him. "There is cereal though." She watched as he pulled out a mixing bowl and dumped a quarter of the cereal box's contents into it for his breakfast. She didn't say a word, although there was a time she would have admonished him for being such a glutton. She finished taking her pills and took out a normal-sized cereal bowl for herself.

Alice looked worse for wear even after a second shower. She was wearing a lot of concealer on her face where she had suffered cuts and blows, and she walked gingerly from her stiffened body parts. She hoped to have the time now to rest her body from the past few days.

"Hey, Mom. Want to go out and play some tennis?" Sean asked when he saw her. She was looking old today, not as bad as Kathy, but moving quite slowly.

"Naaaw," she replied with a smile. "I feel like watching movies today and vegging on the couch. Maybe another time?"

"Yeah, sure. But you always say we've got to keep active..." he teased, enjoying the fact that he could turn her words back on her.

"Yeah, yeah," she waved off his teasing with a smile. "Want to watch movies with us gals?"

"Well, actually..." he began, seeing as he couldn't get a tennis match out of her.

"You want to go play video games? Here or with your pals?" she asked knowingly.

"If you don't mind? Coach has us scheduled every night next week, and I won't get another chance."

Alice exchanged a look with Kathy, who nodded discreetly, and she let the young man go. It was a relief as they could all be themselves after he left without trying to hide how badly they truly felt. Emily joined them on the couch, a cereal bowl held in her hands as she chewed dispiritedly.

"You okay?" Alice asked the teen, worrying that all this had been too much for her.

"Yeah, just tired," she admitted as she used her spoon to shovel in some cereal.

"Yeah, me too," Alice agreed ruefully, watching her daughter from the corner of her eye.

Kathy shook her head. This was such a weird situation to be in. Her wife and daughter were overly tired because they had disposed of bodies this morning! "Who cleaned the fish?" she asked, having seen the fillets in the refrigerator.

"Mom made me," Emily said sullenly as she took another spoonful.

"You caught the biggest fish," Alice grumped and her daughter looked up. They shared a smile.

It took three days before Alice and Emily felt agile enough to walk without pain and stiffness. Emily went with them to Kathy's

appointments, and Alice began to teach her how to stretch before practicing basic karate and other martial arts' moves.

"What are you doing?" Sean asked, seeing what looked like yoga moves.

Alice explained that she was teaching Emily some basic physical defense moves.

Of course, Sean had seen his mother work out in their weight room over the years, but she had never taught any of them her moves before. "She's not going to be able to do squat," he teased his sister.

"Huh, a lot you know. When Mom finishes teaching me, I'll be able to flip you!"

He laughed, but he looked at his mother and asked, "Would you teach me?"

"I don't know, smart guy. You're pretty busy with school sports."

"I'm not always there," he pointed out, wondering if she just didn't want to teach him.

"I could show you a few things, but you have to listen to me. No squirming out of things because you think it's sissy or something." She mentally chastised herself for using the word 'sissy' since it reminded her of something her father would have said. She didn't talk about her father...ever.

Alice took her children through the basic moves, correcting them when they tried to hurry through them, showing them time and time again until they could flawlessly achieve them.

"C'mon, Mom. We have done this five times already today," Sean complained after a week of moves he didn't think had any connection.

"Look, this isn't the Karate Kid with 'shine on, shine off,'" she warned him, looking up at the man that was her son. He still had some filling out

to do, but she could see that football and other sports had really sculpted his young body. "You agreed," she warned him, and he nodded, sighing, and going back to the repetitive moves. "Once you learn these moves, they become instinctive. You'll see," she promised them both.

"How are they doing?" Kathy asked, having heard the kids' complaints when they thought Alice wasn't listening.

"Neither one of them is patient," she admitted, trying not to remember her own training. "I think Emily will have to go to a dojo without me eventually. Maybe when Sean goes off to college next year."

"I don't want to think about that yet. It's a year away. Has he talked about any of the schools he might want to attend?"

Alice shook her head. Nowadays, she didn't talk to the kids except about the moves, slowly building on the foundation of what she had taught them step by step, which was hard as the kids wanted to be breaking wooden boards already.

And Alice wasn't teaching them all the time; she was doing other work. She'd let the gardeners go and placed others in their positions. Kathy had admitted that having assassins as their employees, even unknowingly, had unnerved her. Julio hadn't been pleased, but the routes that Alice had given them—and she hadn't given him all of the routes he knew— compensated him, so there was no resentment. He just liked knowing that people he brought into the country had a way to earn an honest living where he could get them green cards legally. He knew that Alice was right and leaving their posts had been dangerous. Now, he had to make other plans. Alice and he had reached an amicable agreement. The men and women who did their gardens now were part of a local service she had hired, legitimate and above board.

"What do you mean you aren't going to watch her house anymore?" former Senator Edwards asked the man standing before him.

"Look, we've watched her for months. We could watch her for years and nothing would change. She's cost me so much money in new tires it isn't even funny anymore. We have had nothing new to report to you in a very long time. What is the point? Why pay these men to do nothing but sleep in their cars every night outside the Weaver estate?"

"Sleep?" he asked angrily. "I don't pay your men to sleep!"

"It's a figure of speech," he lied, but he knew they slept because he'd caught them a time or two himself. "Enough already, Edwards. What are we watching them for?"

Ken Edwards wasn't certain why he wanted Alice Weaver and her family watched anymore, but he felt it was his decision to fire these people, and they weren't allowed to quit. Much to his chagrin, he had no choice in the matter when they walked off the job. He was furious but unable to do anything about it. He had already called in several old favors and had Alice investigated by the police and the IRS, and she'd gotten off. Now, the FBI was bungling the job, and it made him so angry he could choke.

"Hey, Ken? I have someone I want you to meet," his manager stuck his head in the room, so he could make the introductions. He'd been paid a lot of money under the table to make sure these two met, and he wasn't about to screw it up.

"I don't want to meet anyone," Ken waved him off, lost in thought as he took a drink of the whiskey he favored.

"Believe me, Ken, you want to meet this person," the man put in meaningfully.

"I'm tired. That was a long speech, and those questions were endless," he complained, hating the speeches he had to give, but they paid well, and he could only trade favors so far. Some things cost a lot of money, and he had a lifestyle he wished to maintain.

His manager wouldn't take no for an answer. "Ken Edwards, this is Sandi Pasternack," he said as he ushered Sandi into Ken's suite…

The End ~ for now. ~ 😊 ~

K'ANNE MEINEL

If you have enjoyed **MALEFIC MALICE,** I hope you will enjoy
this excerpt from

Outback Born

A Woman Down Under Series

Best-Selling Fiction Author
K'Anne Meinel

CHAPTER ONE

The heat would have killed a lesser man or woman, but the small group was used to it. They stood there for a moment, each standing on one leg as they waited. Had they sat on the ground or laid down; the heat would have been infinitely worse. The sand was blistering hot to the touch. By standing with only one foot touching the scorching sands at a time, it lessened the amount of fiery heat their bodies had to deal with. The woman and girl watched warily as the male leader chewed thoughtfully before pointing with his chin, grunting out a command, and nodding. A young boy rushed up, just in time for them all to head out again. Resentfully, he sighed at the missed opportunity for a rest. The older man glared warningly at him for a moment, and when the young boy glanced over, he saw a similar look on the older woman and an almost smug look on the young girl's face. She turned and headed out, following the older man, who had immediately turned away.

Moving around a spinifex, the boy startled two lizards sheltering in its welcoming and limited shade. His spear caught one, and he sliced it open neatly, bringing it to his mouth immediately and enjoying the still warm blood, which dripped down his chin as he ate. He rapidly walked on, trying to catch up to the older man but keeping far enough away that he could hunt and protect them.

The older woman, his dam, scooped up the second lizard and crushed its head before she stuffed it in the woven bag slung around her shoulders. The lizard's tail twitched as it was in the throes of dying. She too noticed the heat but in an absent way, the thick soles of her feet

protecting her from its burn as the heat reflected off the red sands. Her eyes traveled around the spinifex, hoping for another lizard and annoyed that her son had been such a glutton and eaten the first. Her eyes scanned the area, looking for other targets, her resentment fading as she began walking rapidly towards where her family had already disappeared.

They spread out attempting to scavenge as much as possible in this sparse and bare territory, out of sight of each other but within hearing distance. The young girl gathered items as she traveled her own path. She looked about the area, not fearful of its enormous expanse. She was unable to see her family but was not afraid since she knew generally where they might be. The family had spread out to hunt and scavenge while traveling over the vast terrain. They were one with their environment, specially adapted to an area not intended to support many, and yet, many lived here, far flung over hundreds of miles. Occasionally, she lifted her head, able to scent her family on the faint breeze. She knew the difference between the scent of prey, the smell of fear, and the common body odors that identified her family.

Alinta heard a sound, and she immediately crouched at the noise, understanding the unique piercing sound, almost like a whistle, was a signal from her sire warning of danger. She held her own woven gathering bag tightly to her side, a carved stick held in a protective pose should she need to defend herself or she was called to defend the family. She balanced the water urn, a small bark vessel, on her head, keeping her neck straight and stiff, so it didn't fall off. Alinta tested the air, smelling for the source of potential danger. She heard the clicking sound of her dam trying to locate her children. Alinta clicked back. It

was short and sweet but delivered in a way that carried on the still air of the desert. She heard a nearly identical sound from her brother at almost the same moment but coming from a different direction. She knew better than to make any other noise, which might give away their location to the danger that held them frozen in the underbrush, possibly scaring off necessary game. After a while, she heard her father make another whistling sound, releasing them from the command to stay hidden and silent while danger was about. Not knowing the source of the danger, Alinta headed out again in the same direction, this time, her senses were heightened, and while she scavenged, she was on high alert for the danger her father had sensed, although she knew she might never know what he had sensed or seen. After all, he certainly wouldn't discuss it with her, a mere girl.

The hours passed as they traveled in a northeasterly direction using ancient paths that only they could see. They avoided traveling on the path itself, instead remaining nearby in order to hunt and gather. Some of these paths were called song trails, named by the elders who understood such things. The people accepted this information without questioning their superior knowledge. The mysticism of these trails was knowledge only given to the elders, and it was passed down from generation to generation.

Alinta found grubs and other insects, which she stuffed in her mouth as she traveled. This was permissible as she hunted for bigger game such as lizards, snakes, and rodents. She also gathered a bundle of sticks, slowly building a pile under one arm while keeping the other hand and arm free to poke and prod and defend with her stick if necessary. Late in the day, her father managed to stun and then kill a

small kangaroo, and they stopped for the day to cook the abundance of meat. He chose a small gully where he could look out on the higher bank. He waited for his son and indicated he was to take another position across the gully on another bank.

Alinta's mother pulled out pieces of fluff she had gathered from small nests and some flint she would use to draw a spark. With a quick and practiced movement, she drew the flint against another stone. She leaned down to blow on the spark that landed in her tinder, puffing gently until the spark turned into a flame. Slowly, she added bits and pieces of smaller twigs and later, some of the wood they had gathered. Finally, they had a small fire to cook their game. Alinta and her mother ran the pelt of the kangaroo across the flame, singeing off the hair. The smell was terrible, but they were accustomed to it and were able to ignore it. None of them would eat the pelt of the animal. Then, her mother raked the coals into a small hole she had dug, and they placed the kangaroo in the hole, piling on more wood, grasses, and leaves, so it would cook thoroughly. As the hours passed, the delicious smell of cooked meat filled the air, dissipating any leftover smell of burnt hair, and finally, her father came down from his guard position on the bank. Her mother pulled back the coals, twigs, burnt grasses, and leaves to reveal the juicy, cooked meat. Alinta tried not to resent her father's gluttony as he ate first, her mother's warning glance cutting off any sign of resentment as Alinta opened her gathering bag, reached in, and began to gnaw on a lizard she pulled out. Her mother contributed more grubs and a snake, and between them they ate. Her brother twitched impatiently from where he still stood watch on the ridge, the aroma of the cooked meat making him hungry. He eventually switched places

with his sire and ate to his heart's content, casting superior looks towards his sister before returning to guard the family.

At a signal from her sire, Alinta's mother cut out a piece of the meat for the two of them using a stone that had been sharpened and chipped on one side. The other side fit in her palm and allowed her to manage the stone. The sizzling of the fat on the coals was loud in the still evening as the fire died down and they ate. Both women wanted to eat more, but Alinta's mother covered the meat, saving some for the next day. The small kangaroo wouldn't last long between two hungry males and two starving females.

The family continued their scavenging in the coming days, only heading back south in their eternal quest to find food and survive on the sparse land when the weather began to change and become colder. Alinta shivered at night, grateful when her mother joined her to share body heat. Her mother was sometimes called to duty, servicing her husband as he attempted to get more children from her aging body. Alinta wondered at this. Her father's rutting seemed to give him pleasure, but her mother's resigned and vacant looks told the young girl she wasn't enjoying the deed, and her brother's amused look confused her.

Alinta didn't understand when her body had begun to change this season. No longer was her body straight and flat. Her flow had come to her, and her breasts had grown. Now, she ached monthly. Her hips were also rounding, and she had become taller. Her mother explained about keeping herself clean and answering a husband's needs when the time came for her to be given to the proper man. She also explained about how to entice a man into becoming aroused. Alinta didn't enjoy

these instructions, finding them embarrassing, and she was relieved when her mother stopped. She was more interested in the plants her mother showed her that helped to relieve the aches and pains her body suffered during her monthly flow.

Her father headed for their ancestral gathering grounds, the bora grounds, signs of other families and other people becoming more obvious as they came closer to the sacred area. A broken twig and a dislodged stone told their tales of others in the vicinity. Her father and brother moved in closer to protect her mother and sister, keeping them constantly in view as they came closer to others. Alinta knew this was because other roving bands of people frequently looked for and captured women for wives. Her mother, while no longer in her prime, could still bear children, so she had value. Alinta, since becoming a woman and having her first flow, was now extremely valuable. Her father grunted out a command to her mother, and Alinta now wore a flap of the kangaroo pelt across her middle, hiding her charms from any who might see her. At night, her father slept closer to them, his spear held in his hand, ready to charge up and defend his daughter, his most valuable asset.

Alinta had been raised in a harsh environment. The desert winds burnished and toughened her skin to the color of dark honey. Centuries of breeding ensured that her skin was darker than some tribes but lighter than others. Her mother's people, lighter than her father's, instilled a cast to her skin that others did not have. Her features were a delicate blend of her parents'. Her nose was finer, and her face was narrower than most in her tribe. Her girlish figure was taking on a woman's curves as her menses changed her from a mere girl into a

woman. Her mother spent a great deal of time explaining about taking care of herself during this important time—how to please her mate, how to be a helpful wife, and what duties were expected of her. Alinta simply accepted this as she knew no better, but a tiny curl of resentment grew within her over the freedoms enjoyed by her brother. He was not watched as closely, and he was able to come and go at will, answerable only to their father, who ruled them all with an iron hand. Alinta was pleased when her mother once again finished explaining her duties. She found them uncomfortable to discuss, and when asked, she had no further questions for her mother. She would accept her fate when she was given to the man her father would eventually choose.

The land seemed to become more arid as they headed to the bora grounds. Finding water was becoming more difficult, but the aboriginal people knew their land and the strata where water flowed below the desert sands. When they needed to fill their water urns, they would stop near the rocks in a place familiar to Alinta's mother, and she would begin to dig using a coolamon, a shallow vessel her mother had pecked out of stone in order to dig in the desert sands. Alinta helped her, pushing the sand away from the hole she was digging. Slowly, inch by inch, foot by foot, she dug down into the hard-packed sands, throwing the sand up on the sides while Alinta pulled it back carefully from the edge. Finally, she began handing up full vessels of sand, which slowly became damp, and Alinta dumped them well away from the hole her mother was in. She handed the coolamon back frequently as they continued to dig. Eventually, they found a bit of bark her mother had buried there previously, and below this they found cool, refreshing water. She handed down her water urn, and her mother

sloshed the water in it until it was full. Alinta took a drink of this cool water before handing down her mother's urn and listening to her fill it. The air of the desert felt cool against her bare skin, the damp sands giving off no heat as the sun set. She carefully put the urns to the side, woven leaves covering their tops to prevent evaporation. Alinta then handed the bark to her mother, who cautiously covered the hole once again and began to push sand back on it to prevent evaporation. Slowly, her mother's head rose from the hole as she stomped the dirt back in place, and Alinta helped her hide the water hole. Together they wiped away all signs of their digging, hiding their source of water from any casual observers.

They quickly took their urns to the campsite Alinta's father had chosen. Alinta handed her father her urn, bowing her head as he took a drink. Her mother offered the same to her son, cutting him off when he would have drunk more than his fair share. Her mother soon had a small fire going where they cooked the mice, lizards, and snakes they had caught that day. The offerings were few and were supplemented with desert fruit, quandongs, and seeds, small things that meant the difference between life and death to the people who lived in this arid region of Australia.

TO BE CONTINUED...

Check out all my books at: www.kannemeinel.com.

About the Author

K'Anne Meinel is a Lesbian Fiction bestselling author with more than 100 published works including shorts, novellas, and novels. She is an American author born in Milwaukee, Wisconsin and raised in Oconomowoc. Upon early graduation from high school she went to a private college in Milwaukee and then moved to California for seventeen years before returning to the state. Many of her stories have Wisconsin in them as settings for her wonderful, realistic, and detailed backgrounds. Named the lesbian Danielle Steel of her time, K'Anne continues to write interesting stories in a variety of genres in both the lesbian and mainstream fiction categories.

~ Because a publisher should stand behind their authors~

What do you do when you meet someone who changes everything you know about love and passion?

Paige Harlow is a good girl. She's always known where she was going in life: top grades, an ivy league school, a medical degree, regular church attendance, and a happy marriage to a man. So falling in love with her gorgeous roommate and best friend Alyssa Torres is no small crisis. Alyssa is chasing demons of her own, a medical condition that makes her an outcast and a family dysfunctional to the point of disintegration make her a questionable choice for any stable relationship. But Paige's heart is no longer her own. She must now battle the prejudices of her family, friends, and church and come to peace with her new sexuality before she can hope to win the affections of the woman of her dreams. But will love be enough?

~ Because a publisher should stand behind their authors~

When Delaney Delacroix is called to locate a missing girl, she never plans on getting caught up with a human trafficking investigation or with the local witch. Meeting with Raelin Montrose changes her life in so many ways that Delaney isn't sure that this isn't destiny.

Raelin Montrose is a practicing Wiccan, and when the ley lines that run under her home tell her that someone is coming, she can't imagine that she was going to solve a mystery and find the love of her life at the same time.

www.shadoepublishing.com

Amelia Gittens had the credit of being the first and only woman thus far in the United States military of being a sniper in combat, made possible by being in the Military Police unit of the crack 10th Mountain Infantry Division. After retirement she joins the City of New York Police Department, and suddenly finds herself involved in a suspect shooting incident which soon encroaches upon her entire life. In order to protect her therapist who has been targeted as a revenge killing, Amelia takes on the responsibility as if she was still in the Army, treating it as a tactical maneuver.

~ Because a publisher should stand behind their authors~

An abused and bullied teenager is suddenly granted great and terrible powers by an ancient goddess. Each step towards womanhood is shaped by her new abilities, as is the woman she will become. Devil or angel, which will she be? Will the woman who chases her ever know for sure?

Both men tried to shoot her then, and the two women were stunned at the speed with which she moved. Penny charged straight at the gunmen then dove under their fire. Spinning on her back she kicked the legs from under one man, and as he fell, she kicked the gun from the other man's hand. Spinning back to the first man she saw the gun barrel moving toward her, and she lashed out with her foot. Her boot crushed his skull and she rolled to her feet to grab the last man in a neck lock. A quick twist and he lay lifeless in her arms.

She let him fall, as, breathing deeply, she came down off combat mode. "Are you ladies all right?" she asked as she untied the ropes that held the older woman.

"Who are you?" asked the old woman fearfully, as she pulled the tape from her mouth.

"They call me Lady Blue," smiled Penny as she helped the woman to stand.

"What are you?" It was the younger woman who spoke.

"Cold, hungry, dead tired, and covered in blue war paint," giggled Penny as she released the older woman's arm. She turned and began to search the bodies.